P9-CBH-963

NO LONGER THE PROPERTY OF
UNIVERSITY OF ARIZONA

KLOSTERHEIM

A Banquo Book
®

PR
4534
K5
1982

KLOSTERHEIM

or: The Masque

By

Thomas De Quincey
"The English Opium-Eater"

With an introduction by John Weeks

Published by
Woodbridge Press Publishing Company
Santa Barbara, California 93111

Published and distributed by
Woodbridge Press Publishing Company
Post Office Box 6189
Santa Barbara, California 93111

New material copyright © 1982 by John Weeks

All rights reserved.

No portion of the new material in this book may be reproduced in any manner without the written consent of the publisher.

Simultaneously published in the United States and Canada

Printed in the United States of America

Library of Congress Cataloging in Publication Data

De Quincey, Thomas, 1785-1859.
    Klosterheim, or, The masque.

    (A Banquo Book)
    Reprint. Originally published: 1832.
    I. Title.
PR4534.K5   1982   823'.8   82-8517
ISBN 0-912800-98-4   AACR2

INTRODUCTION

A curious book appeared in Britain during the spring of 1832. The title page read, "Klosterheim; or, The Masque, By the English Opium-Eater." Despite the cryptic byline, the author was by no means anonymous, for there was only one man in the world who bore that appellation.

He was Thomas De Quincey, 46, one of the Empire's most prominent journalists and the author, ten years earlier, of a sensational autobiography called "Confessions of an English Opium-Eater."

Opium then was plentiful, cheap and perfectly legal. Many distinguished men of the time were addicts, including the poets Samuel Taylor Coleridge and George Crabbe, the politician William Wilberforce, and the lawyer and writer Sir James Mackintosh. These men bore their addiction without ceremony.

De Quincey, 1785-1859, who had begun taking it as a pain-killer when he was still a teenager, was the first to draw broad public attention to opium as an extraordinary and potentially dangerous substance. Writing in an opulent prose-poetry style, he described both the "Pleasures" and the "Pains" of opium, the euphoric dream-reveries it induced as well as the harrowing nightmares of withdrawal.

De Quincey valued both, the pleasures and the pains, a point made explicit in "Suspiria De Profundis," his sequel to "Confessions" published in 1845. In it, he describes his bondage by turns to various symbolic "Ladies of Sorrow," one of whom is "Our Lady of Darkness," or opium. She is the last to take possession of him, and she receives him with the following charge:

v

"See that thy scepter lie heavy on his head ... banish the frailties of hope, wither the relenting of love, scorch the fountains of tears, curse him as only thou canst curse. So shall he see the things that ought *not* to be seen, sights that are abominable, and secrets that are unutterable. So shall he read elder truths, sad truths, grand truths, fearful truths. So shall he rise again *before* he dies. And so shall our commission be accomplished which from God we had—to plague his heart until we had unfolded the capacities of his spirit."

Like Blake, De Quincey believed it is necessary to plumb the darkest depths of experience to rise above them again with full knowledge and complete victory. "Pain driven to agony or grief driven to frenzy, is essential to the ventilation of profound creatures," he wrote, and "without a basis of the dreadful there is no perfect rapture." Only by experiencing the worst that there is in the world can the world be transcended. "The world disappears: I see only the grand relics ... monuments of a wrath that has been reconciled, of a wrong that has been atoned for, convulsions of a storm that has gone by."

De Quincey's bent toward the extremities of experience seems to have been manifest even in his physical appearance. Thomas Carlyle observed of De Quincey that he could have been mistaken "for the beautifullest little child: blue-eyed, sparkling face, had there not been a something, too, which said, '*Eccovi*—this child has been in hell.' "

During his long career, De Quincey yearned to write more of what he called the "Literature of Power," imaginative literature that is timeless, as opposed to what he called the "Literature of Knowledge," topical literature that is subject to revision and obsolescence. But despite his one great success with "Confessions," he was doomed to long toil as a journalist, writing endless periodical pieces which earned him reputation but little income or artistic self-fulfillment.

He had aspirations as a novelist, but he wrote only one, the Gothic romance "Klosterheim." The Scotch publisher William Blackwood had made him a standing offer of a hundred pounds if he would produce a work of fiction, and De Quincey wrote "Klosterheim" to claim the prize. He chose the Gothic form because it was popular, and he no doubt hoped to strike the public fancy again, as he had done a decade earlier with "Confessions."

Gothic fiction, introduced to England in 1765 with Horace Walpole's "Castle of Otranto," dominated the novel for the rest of the century, reaching its apotheosis in the 1790s with Matthew Lewis' "The Monk" and the novels of Ann Radcliffe. Gothic fiction is an extravagant literature of mystery and terror, in which real or supposed supernatural agencies aid in exposing nefarious conspiracies or unavenged crimes. Settings are generally pseudo-medieval, characters are the stereotypical heroes, villains and damsels in distress, and stock props include castles or monasteries with labyrinthine corridors and secret passages.

De Quincey's "Klosterheim," though late to the game, is an archtypal Gothic novel.

The setting is a mythical city called Klosterheim, located in southern Germany during the Thirty Years War (1618-1648). This war, which devastated Germany, began as a conflict between German Protestant nobles and the Catholic Habsburgs of Austria. It erupted into general European war when Sweden and later France entered on the Protestant side, in an attempt to crush the Habsburg empire.

In "Klosterheim," the landgrave or ruler of Klosterheim is a villainous man who has achieved his office by murdering the former landgrave. Though Klosterheim is loyal to the Austrian empire, the landgrave is in secret league with the Swedes, which in effect protects the city from the ravages of war. However, its citizens are tyrannized from within by the landgrave himself.

As the story opens, the Lady Paulina is one among a caravan of citizens traveling under Imperial guard from Vienna to the supposed refuge of Klosterheim. The caravan is attacked just short of its goal by a mercenary host, and though the enemies are driven off, they take captive an Imperial officer named Maximilian, who is the lover of Paulina.

Thereafter, a mysterious figure who calls himself the Masque begins to make strange appearances within the fortified walls of Klosterheim. Wielding what seem to be supernatural powers, he conducts a series of raids which embarrass and outrage the landgrave and his evil lieutenant, Luigi Adorni.

Driven to a desperation of paranoia, the landgrave imprisons Paulina, who is suspected of complicity, and means to execute her. She is saved by the landgrave's own daughter, who is killed instead. Finally, the Masque contrives to steal an entire Imperial army into the city. The landgrave is confronted and exposed and the Masque reveals himself. He is not only Maximilian. He is the son of the murdered former landgrave and thus the rightful heir to Klosterheim.

De Quincey's novel was briefly popular. It was dramatized on the London stage for most of one season. Coleridge praised it warmly, stating in a letter to the publisher that "in purity of style and idiom, in which the Scholar is ever implied, and the scholarly never obtrudes itself, it reaches an excellence to which Sir Walter Scott ... appears never to have aspired."

The book was published in the United States in 1855 with a preface by Shelton Mackenzie, who wrote that the novel "stands among De Quincey's numerous writings as the only complete and extensive effort of his 'imagination all compact.'"

Nevertheless, De Quincey himself directed that "Klosterheim" be omitted from his Collected Works (1853-60), and most of his critics have assumed his motive was shame. But two of his biographers, David Masson and Edward Sackville West, point out that much was omitted from the collection (De Quincey died in 1859 before it was completed) and suggest that in the case of "Klosterheim" De Quincey may have been reluctant to haggle with Blackwood for the copyright.

Whatever the case, and despite the fact that "Klosterheim" finally appeared in 1871 in a supplementary volume of the Collected Works, the novel has all but disappeared from both public and scholarly knowledge.

The book has faults, to be sure. It is populated with caricatures. The dialogue is generally mannered and stiff. There is a general laboriousness and prolixity of syntax which robs the narrative of much animation. Instead of writing "she couldn't help but fear the worst," De Quincey will write, "she could not wean herself from the painful fascination of imagining the very worst possibilities to which their present situation was liable."

But there are also many virtues in "Klosterheim." There are intermittent passages of "impassioned prose," to use one of De Quincey's own favorite phrases, which roll and reverberate like organ music in a cathedral. There are striking images, as one would expect from a man famous for his dreams.

And some of the novel's devices work wonderfully. As the caravan approaches Klosterheim, amidst the suspense of anticipated attack, De Quincey deftly shifts the perspective back and forth, between the anxious refugees catching sight at last of the city, and the Klosterheimers, watching anxiously from the walls. Just as the attack falls, De Quincey rolls in a heavy fog to obscure the view of the Klosterheimers (and the reader). Suspense accelerates as the disembodied sounds of a savage invisible battle rage and then subside. Suddenly the fog lifts and the bloodied but victorious remnants of the caravan stand before the gates. This authorial shifting, obscuring, distorting and unveiling is provocative stagecraft, to say the least.

"Klosterheim" is also emblematic in its way of a primary pattern in De Quincey's art and thought, the pattern of descent into darkness followed by ascent into light, mystery followed by resolution, dread followed by rapture. "Klosterheim" comes to a fictional conclusion similar to the psychic conclusion of "Suspiria De Profundis," with a "wrath that has been reconciled" and a "wrong that has been atoned for."

"Klosterheim" is not only worthy of attention as a neglected curiosity of Gothic fiction and Romantic literature, but as an overlooked source of reference in considering the life and work of Thomas De Quincey. Among his own works, at least, "Klosterheim" deserves more than a century and a half of obscurity, and perhaps it even deserves a place, at least a minor place, among the volumes of the Literature of Power.

— *John Weeks*

CHAPTER I

THE winter of 1633 had set in with unusual severity throughout Suabia and Bavaria, though as yet scarcely advanced beyond the first week of November. It was, in fact, at the point when our tale commences, the eighth of that month, or, in our modern computation, the eighteenth; long after which date it had been customary of late years, under any ordinary state of the weather, to extend the course of military operations, and without much decline of vigor. Latterly, indeed, it had become apparent that entire winter campaigns, without either formal suspensions of hostilities, or even partial relaxations, had entered professedly as a point of policy into the system of warfare which now swept over Germany in full career, threatening soon to convert its vast central provinces—so recently blooming Edens of peace and expanding prosperity—into a howling wilderness; and which had already converted immense tracts into one universal aceldama, or human shambles, reviving to the recollection at every step the extent of past happiness in the endless memorials of its destruction. This innovation upon the old practice of war had been introduced by the Swedish armies, whose northern habits and training had fortunately prepared them to receive a German winter as a very beneficial exchange; whilst upon the less hardy soldiers from Italy, Spain, and the Southern France, to whom the harsh transition from their own sunny skies had made the very same climate a severe trial of constitution, this change of policy pressed with a hardship that sometimes crippled their exertions.

1

It was a change, however, not so long settled as to resist the extraordinary circumstances of the weather. So fierce had been the cold for the last fortnight, and so premature, that a pretty confident anticipation had arisen, in all quarters throughout the poor exhausted land, of a general armistice. And as this, once established, would offer a ready opening to some measure of permanent pacification, it could not be surprising that the natural hopefulness of the human heart, long oppressed by gloomy prospects, should open with unusual readiness to the first colorable dawn of happier times. In fact, the reaction in the public spirits was sudden and universal. It happened also that the particular occasion of this change of prospect brought with it a separate pleasure on its own account. Winter, which by its peculiar severity had created the apparent necessity for an armistice, brought many household pleasures in its train—associated immemorially with that season in all northern climates. The cold, which had casually opened a path to more distant hopes, was also for the present moment a screen between themselves and the enemy's sword. And thus it happened that the same season, which held out a not improbable picture of final restoration, however remote, to public happiness, promised them a certain foretaste of this blessing in the immediate security of their homes.

But in the ancient city of Klosterheim it might have been imagined that nobody participated in these feelings. A stir and agitation amongst the citizens had been conspicuous for some days; and on the morning of the eighth, spite of the intense cold, persons of every rank were seen crowding from an early hour to the city walls, and returning homewards at intervals, with anxious and dissatisfied looks. Groups of both sexes were collected at every corner of the wider streets, keenly debating, or angrily protesting; at one time denouncing vengeance to some great enemy; at another, passionately lamenting some past or half-forgotten calamity, recalled to their thoughts whilst anticipating a similar catastrophe for the present day.

Above all, the great square, upon which the ancient castellated palace or *schloss* opened by one of its fronts, as well as a principal convent of the city, was the resort of many turbulent spirits. Most of these were young men, and amongst them many students of the university: for the war, which had thinned or totally dispersed some of the greatest universities in Germany, under the particular circumstances of its situation, had greatly increased that of Klosterheim. Judging by the tone which prevailed, and the random expressions which fell upon the ear at intervals, a stranger might conjecture that it was no empty lamentation over impending evils which occupied this crowd, but some serious preparation for meeting or redressing them. An officer of some distinction had been for some time observing them from the antique portals of the palace. It was probable, however, that little more than their gestures had reached him; for at length he moved nearer, and gradually insinuated himself into the thickest part of the mob, with the air of one who took no further concern in their proceedings than that of simple curiosity. But his martial air and his dress allowed him no means of covering his purpose. With more warning and leisure to arrange his precautions, he might have passed as an indifferent spectator; as it was, his jewel-hilted sabre, the massy gold chain, depending in front from a costly button and loop which secured it half way down his back, and his broad crimson scarf, embroidered in a style of peculiar splendor, announced him as a favored officer of the Landgrave, whose ambitious pretensions, and tyrannical mode of supporting them, were just now the objects of general abhorrence in Klosterheim. His own appearance did not belie the service which he had adopted. He was a man of stout person, somewhat elegantly formed, in age about three or four and thirty, though perhaps a year or two of his apparent age might be charged upon the bronzing effects of sun and wind. In bearing and carriage he announced to every eye the mixed carelessness and self-possession of a military training; and as his features were regular, and remarkably intelligent, he would have been pronounced, on the whole, a man of winning exterior, were it not for the repulsive effect of his eye, in which there was a sinister expression of treachery, and at times a ferocious one of cruelty.

Placed upon their guard by his costume, and the severity of his countenance, those of the lower rank were silent as he moved along, or lowered their voices into whispers and inaudible murmurs. Amongst the students, however, whenever they happened to muster strongly, were many fiery young men, who disdained to temper the expression of their feelings, or to moderate their tone. A large group of these at one corner of the square drew attention upon themselves, as well by the conspicuous station which they occupied upon the steps of a church portico, as by the loudness of their voices. Towards them the officer directed his steps; and probably no lover of *scenes* would have had very long to wait for some explosion between parties both equally ready to take offence, and careless of giving it; but at that moment, from an opposite angle of the square, was seen approaching a young man in plain clothes, who drew off the universal regard of the mob upon himself, and by the uproar of welcome which saluted him occasioned all other sounds to be stifled. "Long life to our noble leader!"—"Welcome to the good Max!" resounded through the square. "Hail to our noble brother!" was the acclamation of the students. And everybody hastened forward to meet him with an impetuosity which for the moment drew off all attention from the officer: he was left standing by himself on the steps of the church, looking down upon this scene of joyous welcome—the sole spectator who neither fully understood its meaning, nor shared in its feelings.

The stranger, who wore in part the antique costume of the university of Klosterheim, except where he still retained underneath a travelling dress, stained with recent marks of the roads and the weather, advanced amongst his friends with an air at once frank, kind, and dignified. He replied to their greetings in the language of cheerfulness; but his features expressed anxiety, and his manner was hurried. Whether he had not observed the officer overlooking them, or thought that the importance of the communications which he had to make transcended all common restraints of caution, there was little time to judge; so it was, at any rate, that, without lowering his voice, he entered abruptly upon his business.

"Friends! I have seen the accursed Holkerstein; I have penetrated within his fortress. With my own eyes I have viewed and numbered his vile assassins. They are in strength triple the utmost amount of our friends. Without help from us, our kinsmen are lost. Scarce one of us but will lose a dear friend before three nights are over, should Klosterheim not resolutely do her duty."

"She shall, she shall!" exclaimed a multitude of voices.

"Then, friends, it must be speedily; never was there more call for sudden resolution. Perhaps, before tomorrow's sun shall set, the sword of this detested robber will be at their throats. For he has some intelligence (whence I know not, nor how much) of their approach. Neither think that Holkerstein is a man acquainted with any touch of mercy or relenting. Where no ransom is to be had, he is in those circumstances that he will and must deliver himself from the burden of prisoners by a general massacre. Infants even will not be spared."

Many women had by this time flocked to the outer ring of the listening audience. And, perhaps, for *their* ears in particular it was that the young stranger urged these last circumstances; adding,

"Will you look down tamely from your city walls upon such another massacre of the innocents as we have once before witnessed?"

"Cursed be Holkerstein!" said a multitude of voices.

"And cursed be those that openly or secretly support him!" added one of the students, looking earnestly at the officer.

"Amen!" said the officer, in a solemn tone, and looking round him with the aspect of one who will not suppose himself to have been included in the suspicion.

"And, friends, remember this," pursued the popular favorite; "whilst you are discharging the first duties of Christians and brave men to those who are now throwing themselves upon the hospitality of your city, you will also be acquitting yourselves of a great debt to the emperor."

"Softly, young gentleman, softly," interrupted the officer; "his serene highness, my liege lord and yours, governs here, and the emperor has no part in our allegiance. For debts, what the city owes to the emperor she will pay. But men and horses, I take it—"

"Are precisely the coin which the time demands; these will best please the emperor, and, perhaps, will suit the circumstances of the city. But, leaving the emperor's rights as a question for lawyers, you, sir, are a soldier,—I question not, a brave one,—will you advise his highness the Landgrave to look down from the castle windows upon a vile marauder, stripping or murdering the innocent people who are throwing themselves upon the hospitality of this ancient city?"

"Ay, sir, that will I, be you well assured—the Landgrave is my sovereign—"

"Since when? Since Thursday week, I think; for so long it is since your *tertia* first entered Klosterheim. But in that as you will, and if it be a point of honor with you gentlemen Walloons to look on whilst women and children are butchered. For such a purpose no man is *my* sovereign; and as to the Landgrave in particular—"

"Nor ours, nor ours!" shouted a tumult of voices, which drowned the young student's words about the Landgrave, though apparently part of them reached the officer. He looked round in quest of some military comrades who might support him in the *voye du fait*, to which, at this point, his passion prompted him. But, seeing none, he exclaimed "Citizens, press not this matter too far—and you, young man, especially, forbear,— you tread upon the brink of treason!"

A shout of derision threw back his words.

"Of treason, I say," he repeated, furiously; "and such wild behavior it is (and I say it with pain) that perhaps even now is driving his highness to place your city under martial law."

"Martial law! did you hear that?" ran along from mouth to mouth.

"Martial law, gentlemen, I say; how will you relish the little articles of that code? The provost marshal makes short leave-takings. Two fathom of rope, and any of these pleasant old balconies which I see around me (pointing, as he spoke, to the antique galleries of wood which ran round the middle stories in the Convent of St. Peter), with a confessor, or none, as the provost's breakfast may chance to allow, have cut short, to my knowledge, the freaks of many a better fellow than any I now see before me."

Saying this, he bowed with a mock solemnity all round to the crowd, which, by this time, had increased in number and violence. Those who were in the outermost circles, and beyond the distinct hearing of what he said, had been discussing with heat the alarming confirmation of their fears in respect to Holkerstein, or listening to the impassioned narrative of a woman, who had already seen one of her sons butchered by this ruffian's people under the walls of the city, and was now anticipating the same fate for her last surviving son and daughter, in case they should happen to be amongst the party now expected from Vienna. She had just recited the tragical circumstances of her son's death, and had worked powerfully upon the sympathizing passions of the crowd, when, suddenly, at a moment so unseasonable for the officer, some imperfect repetition of his words about the provost martial and the rope passed rapidly from mouth to mouth. It was said that he had threatened every man with instant death at the drum-head, who should but speculate on assisting his friends outside, under the heaviest extremities of danger or of outrage. The sarcastic bow and the inflamed countenance of the officer were seen by glimpses further than his words extended. Kindling eyes and lifted arms of many amongst the mob, and chiefly of those on the outside, who had heard his words the most imperfectly, proclaimed to such as knew Klosterheim and its temper at this moment the danger in which he stood. Maximilian, the young student, generously forgot his indignation in concern for his immediate safety. Seizing him by the hand, he exclaimed,

"Sir, but a moment ago you warned me that I stood on the brink of treason: look to your own safety at present; for the eyes of some whom I see yonder are dangerous."

"Young gentleman," the other replied, contemptuously, "I presume that you are a student; let me counsel you to go back to your books. There you will be in your element. For myself, I am familiar with faces as angry as these—and hands something more formidable. Believe me, I see nobody here," and he affected to speak with imperturbable coolness, but his voice became tremulous with passion "whom I can even esteem worthy of a soldier's consideration."

"And yet, Colonel von Aremberg, there is at least one man here who has had the honor of commanding men as elevated as yourself." Saying which, he hastily drew from his bosom, where it hung suspended from his neck, a large flat tablet of remarkably beautiful onyx, on one side of which was sculptured a very striking face; but on the other, which he presented to the gaze of the colonel, was a fine representation of an eagle grovelling on the dust, and beginning to expand its wings—with the single word *Resurgam* by way of motto.

Never was revulsion of feeling so rapidly expressed on any man's countenance. The colonel looked but once; he caught the image of the bird trailing its pinions in the dust, he heard the word *Resurgam* audibly pronounced; his color fled, his lips grew livid with passion; and, furiously unsheathing his sword, he sprung, with headlong forgetfulness of time and place, upon his calm antagonist. With the advantage of perfect self-possession, Maximilian found it easy to parry the tempestuous blows of the colonel; and he would, perhaps, have found it easy to disarm him. But at this moment the crowd, who had been with great difficulty repressed by the more thoughtful amongst the students, burst through all restraints. In the violent outrage offered to their champion and leader, they saw naturally a full confirmation of the worst impressions they had received as to the colonel's temper and intention. A number of them rushed forward to execute a summary vengeance; and the foremost amongst these, a mechanic of Klosterheim, distinguished for his herculean strength, with one blow stretched Von Aremberg on the ground. A savage yell announced the dreadful fate which impended over the fallen officer. And, spite of the generous exertions made for his protection by Maximilian and his brother students, it is probable that at that moment no human interposition could have availed to turn aside the awakened appetite for vengeance, and that he must have perished, but for the accident which at that particular instant of time occurred to draw off the attention of the mob.

A signal gun from a watch-tower, which always in those unhappy times announced the approach of strangers, had been fired about ten minutes before; but, in the turbulent uproar of the crowd, it had passed unnoticed. Hence it was, that, without previous warning to the mob assembled at this point, a mounted courier now sprung into the square at full gallop on his road to the palace, and was suddenly pulled up by the dense masses of human beings.

"News, news!" exclaimed Maximilian; "tidings of our dear friends from Vienna!" This he said with the generous purpose of diverting the infuriated mob from the unfortunate Von Aremberg, though himself apprehending that the courier had arrived from another quarter. His plan succeeded; the mob rushed after the horseman, all but two or three of the most sanguinary, who, being now separated from all assistance, were easily drawn off from their prey. The opportunity was eagerly used to carry off the colonel, stunned and bleeding, within the gates of a Franciscan convent. He was consigned to the medical care of the holy fathers; and Maximilian, with his companions, then hurried away to the chancery of the palace, whither the courier had proceeded with his despatches.

These were interesting in the highest degree. It had been doubted by many, and by others a pretended doubt had been raised to serve the Landgrave's purpose, whether the great cavalcade from Vienna would be likely to reach the entrance of the forest for a week or more. Certain news had now arrived, and was published before it could be stifled, that they and all their baggage, after a prosperous journey so far, would be assembled at that point on this very evening. The courier had left the advanced guard about noonday, with an escort of four hundred of the Black Yagers from the Imperial Guard, and two hundred of Papenheim's Dragoons, at Waldenhausen, on the very brink of the forest. The main body and rear were expected to reach the same point in four or five hours; and the whole party would then fortify their encampment as much as possible against the night attack which they had too much reason to apprehend.

This was news which, in bringing a respite of forty-eight hours, brought relief to some who had feared that even this very night might present them with the spectacle of their beloved friends engaged in a bloody struggle at the very gates of Klosterheim; for it was the fixed resolution of the Landgrave to suffer no diminution of his own military strength, or of the means for recruiting it hereafter. Men, horses, arms, all alike were rigorously laid under embargo by the existing government of the city and such was the military power at its disposal, reckoning not merely the numerical strength in troops, but also the power of sweeping the main streets of the town, and several of the principal roads outside, that it was become a matter of serious doubt whether the unanimous insurrection of the populace had a chance for making head against the government. But others found not even a momentary comfort in this account. They considered that, perhaps, Waldenhausen might be the very ground selected for the murderous attack. There was here a solitary post-house, but no town, or even village. The forest at this point was just thirty-four miles broad; and if the bloodiest butchery should be going on under cover of night, no rumor of it could be borne across the forest in time to alarm the many anxious friends who would this night be lying awake in Klosterheim.

A slight circumstance served to barb and point the public distress, which otherwise seemed previously to have reached its utmost height. The courier had brought a large budget of letters to private individuals throughout Klosterheim; many of these were written by children unacquainted with the dreadful catastrophe which threatened them. Most of them had been long separated, by the fury of the war, from their parents. They had assembled, from many different quarters, at Vienna, in order to join what might be called, in Oriental phrase, *the caravan.* Their parents had also, in many instances, from places equally dispersed, assembled at Klosterheim; and, after great revolutions of fortune, they were now going once more to rejoin each other. Their letters expressed the feelings of hope and affectionate pleasure suitable to the occasion. They retraced the perils they had passed during the twenty-six days of their journey,—the great towns, heaths, and forests, they had traversed since leaving the gates of Vienna; and expressed, in the innocent terms of childhood, the pleasure they felt in having come within two stages of the gates of Klosterheim. "In the forest," said they, "there will be no more dangers to pass; no soldiers; nothing worse than wild deer."

Letters written in these terms, contrasted with the mournful realities of the case, sharpened the anguish of fear and suspense throughout the whole city; and Maximilian with his friends, unable to bear the loud expression of the public feelings, separated themselves from the tumultuous crowds, and adjourning to the seclusion of their college rooms, determined to consult, whilst it was yet not too late, whether, in their hopeless situation

for openly resisting the Landgrave without causing as
much slaughter as they sought to prevent, it might not
yet be possible for them to do something in the way of
resistance to the bloody purposes of Holkerstein.

CHAPTER II

THE travelling party, for whom so much anxiety was
felt in Klosterheim, had this evening reached Waldenhausen without loss or any violent alarm; and, indeed, considering the length of their journey, and the
distracted state of the empire, they had hitherto
travelled in remarkable security. It was now nearly a
month since they had taken their departure from
Vienna, at which point considerable numbers had assembled from the adjacent country to take the benefit of
their convoy. Some of these they had dropped at different turns in their route, but many more had joined
them as they advanced; for in every considerable city
they found large accumulations of strangers, driven in
for momentary shelter from the storm of war as it
spread over one district after another; and many of
these were eager to try the chances of a change, or,
upon more considerate grounds, preferred the protection of a place situated like Klosterheim, in a nook as yet
unvisited by the scourge of military execution. Hence it
happened, that from a party of seven hundred and fifty,
with an escort of four hundred yagers, which was the
amount of their numbers on passing through the gates
of Vienna, they had gradually swelled into a train of
sixteen hundred, including two companies of dragoons,
who had joined them by the emperor's orders at one of
the fortified posts.

It was felt, as a circumstance of noticeable singularity, by most of the party, that, after traversing a large part of Germany without encountering any very imminent peril, they should be first summoned to unusual vigilance, and all the most jealous precautions of fear, at the very termination of their journey. In all parts of their route they had met with columns of troops pursuing their march, and now and then with roving bands of deserters, who were formidable to the unprotected traveller. Some they had overawed by their display of military strength; from others, in the imperial service, they had received cheerful assistance; and any Swedish corps, which rumor had presented as formidable by their numbers, they had, with some exertion of forethought and contrivance, constantly evaded, either by a little detour, or by a temporary halt in some place of strength. But now it was universally known that they were probably waylaid by a desperate and remorseless freebooter, who, as he put his own trust exclusively in the sword, allowed nobody to hope for any other shape of deliverance.

Holkerstein, the military robber, was one of the many monstrous growths which had arisen upon the ruins of social order in this long and unhappy war. Drawing to himself all the malcontents of his own neighborhood, and as many deserters from the regular armies in the centre of Germany as he could tempt to his service by the license of unlimited pillage, he had rapidly created a respectable force; had possessed himself of various castles in Wirtemberg, within fifty or sixty miles of Klosterheim; had attacked and defeated many parties of regular troops sent out to reduce him; and, by great activity and local knowledge, had raised himself to so much consideration, that the terror of his name had spread even to Vienna, and the escort of yagers had been granted by the imperial government as much on his account as for any more general reason. A lady, who was in some way related to the emperor's family, and, by those who were in the secret, was reputed to be the emperor's natural daughter, accompanied the travelling party, with a suite of female attendants. To this lady, who was known by the name of the Countess Paulina, the rest of the company held themselves indebted for their escort; and hence, as much as for her rank, she was treated with ceremonious respect throughout the journey.

The Lady Paulina travelled with her suite in coaches, drawn by the most powerful artillery horses that could be furnished at the various military posts. On this day she had been in the rear; and having been delayed by an accident, she was waited for with some impatience by the rest of the party, the latest of whom had reached Waldenhausen early in the afternoon. It was sunset before her train of coaches arrived; and, as the danger from Holkerstein commenced about this point, they were immediately applied to the purpose of strengthening their encampment against a night attack, by chaining them, together with all the baggage-carts, in a triple line, across the different avenues which seemed most exposed to a charge of cavalry. Many other preparations were made; the yagers and dragoons made arrangements for mounting with ease on the first alarm; strong outposts were established; sentinels posted all round the encampment, who were duly relieved every hour, in consideration of the extreme cold; and, upon the whole, as many veteran officers were amongst them, the great body of the travellers were now able to apply themselves to the task of preparing their evening refreshments with some degree of comfort; for the elder part of the company saw that every precaution had been taken, and the younger were not aware of any extraordinary danger.

Waldenhausen had formerly been a considerable village. At present there was no more than one house,
surrounded, however, by such a large establishment of
barns, stables, and other outhouses, that, at a little distance, it wore the appearance of a tolerable hamlet.
Most of the outhouses, in their upper stories, were filled
with hay or straw; and there the women and children
prepared their couches for the night, as the warmest
resorts in so severe a season. The house was furnished
in the plainest style of a farmer's; but in other respects it
was of a superior order, being roomy and extensive.
The best apartment had been reserved for the Lady
Paulina and her attendants; one for the officers of most
distinction in the escort or amongst the travellers; the
rest had been left to the use of the travellers indiscriminately.

In passing through the hall of entrance, Paulina had
noticed a man of striking and *farouche* appearance,—
hair black and matted, eyes keen and wild, and beaming
with malicious cunning, who surveyed her as she passed
with a mixed look of insolence and curiosity, that involuntarily made her shrink. He had been half reclining
carelessly against the wall, when she first entered, but
rose upright with a sudden motion as she passed him—
not probably from any sentiment of respect, but under
the first powerful impression of surprise on seeing a
young woman of peculiarly splendid figure and impressive beauty, under circumstances so little according with
what might be supposed her natural pretensions. The
dignity of her deportment, and the numbers of her attendants, sufficiently proclaimed the luxurious accom-
modations which her habits might have taught her to
expect; and she was now entering a dwelling which of
late years had received few strangers of her sex, and
probably none but those of the lowest rank.

"Know your distance, fellow!" exclaimed one of the

waiting-women, angrily, noticing his rude gaze and the effect upon her mistress.

"Good faith, madam, I would that the distance between us were more; it was no prayers of mine, I promise you, that brought upon me a troop of horses to Waldenhausen, enough in one twelve hours to eat me out a margrave's ransom. Light thanks I reckon on from yagers; and the payments of dragoons will pass current for as little in the forest, as a lady's frown in Waldenhausen."

"Churl!" said an officer of dragoons, "how know you that our payments are light? The emperor takes nothing without payment; surely not from such as you. But *à propos* of ransoms, what now might be Holkerstein's ransom for a farmer's barns stuffed with a three years' crop?"

"How mean you by that, captain? The crop's my own, and never was in worse hands than my own. God send it no worse luck to-day!"

"Come, come, sir, you understand me better than that; nothing at Waldenhausen, I take it, is yours or any man's, unless by license from Holkerstein. And when I see so many goodly barns and garners, with their jolly charges of hay and corn, that would feed one of Holkerstein's garrisons through two sieges, I know what to think of him who has saved them scot-free. He that serves a robber must do it on a robber's terms. To such bargains there goes but one word, and that is the robber's. But, come, man, I am not thy judge. Only I would have my soldiers on their guard at one of Holkerstein's outposts. And thee, farmer, I would have to remember that an emperor's grace may yet stand thee instead, when a robber is past helping thee to a rope."

The soldiers laughed, but took their officer's hint to watch the motions of a man, whose immunity from spoil, in circumstances so tempting to a military robber's

cupidity, certainly argued some collusion with Holkerstein.

The Lady Paulina had passed on during this dialogue
into an inner room, hoping to have found the quiet and
the warmth which were now become so needful to her
repose. But the antique stove was too much out of repair to be used with benefit; the wood-work was decayed, and admitted currents of cold air; and, above all,
from the slightness of the partitions, the noise and
tumult in a house occupied by soldiers and travellers
proved so incessant, that, after taking refreshments with
her attendants, she resolved to adjourn for the night to
her coach; which afforded much superior resources,
both in warmth and in freedom from noise.

The carriage of the countess was one of those which
had been posted at an angle of the encampment, and on
that side terminated the line of defences; for a deep
mass of wood, which commenced where the carriages
ceased, seemed to present a natural protection on that
side against the approach of cavalry; in reality, from the
quantity of tangled roots, and the inequalities of the
ground, it appeared difficult for a single horseman to
advance even a few yards without falling. And upon this
side it had been judged sufficient to post a single sentinel.

Assured by the many precautions adopted, and by the
cheerful language of the officer on guard, who attended
her to the carriage door, Paulina, with one attendant,
took her seat in the coach, where she had the means of
fencing herself sufficiently from the cold by the weighty
robes of minever and ermine which her ample wardrobe afforded; and the large dimensions of the coach
enabled her to turn it to the use of a sofa or couch.

Youth and health sleep well; and with all the means
and appliances of the Lady Paulina, wearied besides as
she had been with the fatigue of a day's march, per-

formed over roads almost impassable from roughness, there was little reason to think that she would miss the benefit of her natural advantages. Yet sleep failed to come, or came only by fugitive snatches, which presented her with tumultuous dreams,—sometimes of the emperor's court in Vienna, sometimes of the vast succession of troubled scenes and fierce faces that had passed before her since she had quitted that city. At one moment she beheld the travelling equipages and far-stretching array of her own party, with their military escort filing off by torchlight under the gateway of ancient cities; at another, the ruined villages, with their dismantled cottages,—doors and windows torn off, walls scorched with fire, and a few gaunt dogs, with a wolf-like ferocity in their bloodshot eyes, prowling about the ruins,—objects that had really so often afflicted her heart. Waking from those distressing spectacles, she would fall into a fitful doze, which presented her with remembrances still more alarming: bands of fierce deserters, that eyed her travelling party with a savage rapacity which did not confess any powerful sense of inferiority; and in the very fields which they had once cultivated, now silent and tranquil from utter desolation, the mouldering bodies of the unoffending peasants, left unhonored with the rites of sepulture, in many places from the mere extermination of the whole rural population of their neighborhood. To these succeeded a wild chaos of figures, in which the dress and tawny features of Bohemian gypsies conspicuously prevailed, just as she had seen them of late making war on all parties alike; and, in the person of their leader, her fancy suddenly restored to her a vivid resemblance of their suspicious host at their present quarters, and of the malicious gaze with which he had disconcerted her.

A sudden movement of the carriage awakened her, and, by the light of a lamp suspended from a projecting bough of a tree, she beheld, on looking out, the sallow countenance of the very man whose image had so recently infested her dreams. The light being considerably nearer to him than to herself, she could see without being distinctly seen; and, having already heard the very strong presumptions against this man's honesty which had been urged by the officer, and without reply from the suspected party, she now determined to watch him.

CHAPTER III

THE night was pitch dark, and Paulina felt a momentary terror creep over her as she looked into the massy blackness of the dark alleys which ran up into the woods, forced into deeper shade under the glare of the lamps from the encampment. She now reflected with some alarm that the forest commenced at this point, stretching away (as she had been told) in some directions upwards of fifty miles; and that, if the post occupied by their encampment should be inaccessible on this side to cavalry, it might, however, happen that persons with the worst designs could easily penetrate on foot from the concealments of the forest; in which case she herself, and the splendid booty of her carriage, might be the first and easiest prey. Even at this moment, the very worst of those atrocious wretches whom the times had produced might be lurking in concealment, with their eyes fastened upon the weak or exposed parts of the encampment, and waiting until midnight should have buried the majority of their wearied party into the profoundest repose, in order then to make a combined and murderous attack. Under the advantages of sudden surprise and darkness, together with the knowledge which they would not fail to possess of every road and by-path in the woods, it could scarcely be doubted that they might strike a very effectual blow at the Vienna caravan, which had else so nearly completed their journey without loss or memorable privations;—and the knowledge which Holkerstein possessed of the short limits within which his opportunities were now circumscribed would doubtless prompt him to some bold and energetic effort.

Thoughts unwelcome as these Paulina found leisure to pursue; for the ruffian landlord had disappeared almost at the same moment when she first caught a glimpse of him. In the deep silence which succeeded, she could not wean herself from the painful fascination of imagining the very worst possibilities to which their present situation was liable. She imaged to herself the horrors of a *camisade*, as she had often heard it described; she saw, in apprehension, the savage band of confederate butchers, issuing from the profound solitudes of the forest, in white shirts drawn over their armor; she seemed to read the murderous features, lighted up by the gleam of lamps—the stealthy step, and the sudden gleam of sabres; then the yell of assault, the scream of agony, the camp floating with blood; the fury, the vengeance, the pursuit;—all these circumstances of scenes at that time too familiar to Germany passed rapidly before her mind.

But after some time, as the tranquillity continued, her nervous irritation gave way to less agitating but profound sensibilities. Whither was her lover withdrawn from her knowledge? and why? and for how long a time? What an age it seemed since she had last seen him at Vienna! That the service upon which he was employed would prove honorable, she felt assured. But was it dangerous? Alas! in Germany there was none otherwise. Would it soon restore him to her society?

And why had he been of late so unaccountably silent? Or again, *had* he been silent? Perhaps his letters had been intercepted,—nothing, in fact, was more common at that time. The rarity was, if by any accident a letter reached its destination. From one of the worst solicitudes incident to such a situation Paulina was, however, delivered by her own nobility of mind, which raised her above the meanness of jealousy. Whatsoever might have happened, or into whatever situations her lover might have been thrown, she felt no fear that the fidelity of his attachment could have wandered or faltered for a moment; that worst of pangs the Lady Paulina was raised above, equally by her just confidence in herself and in her lover. But yet, though faithful to her, might he not be ill? Might he not be languishing in some one of the many distresses incident to war? Might he not even have perished?

That fear threw her back upon the calamities and horrors of war; and insensibly her thoughts wandered round to the point from which they had started, of her own immediate situation. Again she searched with penetrating eyes the black avenues of the wood as they lay forced almost into strong relief and palpable substance by the glare of the lamps. Again she fancied to herself the murderous hearts and glaring eyes which even now might be shrouded by the silent masses of forest which stretched before her,—when suddenly a single light shot its rays from what appeared to be a considerable distance in one of the avenues. Paulina's heart beat fast at this alarming spectacle. Immediately after, the light was shaded, or in some way disappeared. But this gave the more reason for terror. It was now clear that human beings were moving in the woods. No public road lay in that direction; nor, in so unpopulous a region, could it be imagined that travellers were likely at that time to be abroad. From their own encampment nobody could have any motive for straying to a distance on so severe a night, and at a time when he would reasonably draw upon himself the danger of being shot by the night-guard.

This last consideration reminded Paulina suddenly, as of a very singular circumstance, that the appearance of the light had been followed by no challenge from the sentinel. And then first she remembered that for some time she had ceased to hear the sentinel's step, or the rattle of his bandoleers. Hastily looking along the path, she discovered too certainly that the single sentinel posted on that side of their encampment was absent from his station. It might have been supposed that he had fallen asleep from the severity of the cold; but in that case the lantern which he carried attached to his breast would have continued to burn; whereas all traces of light had vanished from the path which he perambulated. The error was now apparent to Paulina, both in having appointed no more than one sentinel to this quarter, and also in the selection of his beat. There had been frequent instances throughout this war in which by means of a net, such as that carried by the Roman *retiarius* in the contests of the gladiators, and dexterously applied by two persons from behind, a sentinel had been suddenly muffled, gagged, and carried off, without much difficulty. For such a purpose it was clear that the present sentinel's range, lying by the margin of a wood from which his minutest movements could be watched at leisure by those who lay in utter darkness themselves, afforded every possible facility. Paulina scarcely doubted that he had been indeed carried off, in some such way, and not impossibly almost whilst she was looking on.

She would now have called aloud, and have alarmed the camp; but at the very moment when she let down the glass the savage landlord reappeared, and, menac-

ing her with a pistol, awed her into silence. He bore
upon his head a moderate-sized trunk, or portmanteau,
which appeared, by the imperfect light, to be that in
which some despatches had been lodged from the imperial government to different persons in Klosterheim.
This had been cut from one of the carriages in her suite;
and her anxiety was great on recollecting that, from
some words of the emperor's, she had reason to believe
one, at least, of the letters which it conveyed to be in
some important degree connected with the interests of
her lover. Satisfied, however, that he would not find it
possible to abscond with so burdensome an article in any
direction that could save him from instant pursuit and
arrest, she continued to watch for the moment when she
might safely raise the alarm. But great was her consternation when she saw a dark figure steal from a thicket,
receive the trunk from the other, and instantly retreat
into the deepest recesses of the forest.

Her fears now gave way to the imminence of so important a loss; and she endeavored hastily to open the
window of the opposite door. But this had been so effectually barricaded against the cold, that she failed in her
purpose, and, immediately turning back to the other
side, she called, loudly,—"Guard! guard!" The press of
carriages, however, at this point, so far deadened her
voice, that it was some time before the alarm reached
the other side of the encampment distinctly enough to
direct their motions to her summons. Half a dozen yagers and an officer at length presented themselves; but
the landlord had disappeared, she knew not in what
direction. Upon explaining the circumstances of the
robbery, however, the officer caused his men to light a
number of torches, and advance into the wood. But the
ground was so impracticable in most places, from
tangled roots and gnarled stumps of trees, that it was
with difficulty they could keep their footing. They were

also embarrassed by the crossing shadows from the innumerable boughs above them; and a situation of greater perplexity for effective pursuit it was scarcely possible to imagine. Everywhere they saw alleys, arched high overhead, and resembling the aisles of a cathedral, as much in form as in the perfect darkness which reigned in both at this solemn hour of midnight, stretching away apparently without end, but more and more obscure, until impenetrable blackness terminated the long vista. Now and then a dusky figure was seen to cross at some distance; but these were probably deer; and when loudly challenged by the yagers, no sound replied but the vast echoes of the forest. Between these interminable alleys, which radiated as from a centre at this point, there were generally thickets interposed. Sometimes the wood was more open, and clear of all undergrowth—shrubs, thorns, or brambles—for a considerable distance, so that a single file of horsemen might have penetrated for perhaps half a mile; but belts of thicket continually checked their progress, and obliged them to seek their way back to some one of the long vistas which traversed the woods between the frontiers of Suabia and Bavaria.

In this perplexity of paths, the officer halted his party to consider of his further course. At this moment one of the yagers protested that he had seen a man's hat and face rise above a thicket of bushes, apparently not more than a hundred and fifty yards from their own position. Upon that the party were ordered to advance a little, and to throw in a volley, as nearly as could be judged, into the very spot pointed out by the soldier. It seemed that he had not been mistaken; for a loud laugh of derision rose immediately a little to the left of the bushes. The laughter swelled upon the silence of the night, and in the next moment was taken up by another on the right, which again was echoed by a third on the rear. Peal after peal of tumultuous and scornful laughter resounded from the remote solitudes of the forest; and the officer stood aghast to hear this proclamation of defiance from a multitude of enemies, where he had anticipated no more than the very party engaged in the robbery.

To advance in pursuit seemed now both useless and dangerous. The laughter had probably been designed expressly to distract his choice of road at a time when the darkness and intricacies of the ground had already made it sufficiently indeterminate. In which direction, out of so many whence he had heard the sounds, a pursuit could be instituted with any chance of being effectual, seemed now as hopeless a subject of deliberation as it was possible to imagine. Still, as he had been made aware of the great importance attached to the trunk, which might very probably contain despatches interesting to the welfare of Klosterheim, and the whole surrounding territory, he felt grieved to retire with out some further attempt for its recovery. And he stood for a few moments irresolutely debating with himself, or listening to the opinions of his men.

His irresolution was very abruptly terminated. All at once, upon the main road from Klosterheim, at an angle about half a mile ahead where it first wheeled into sight from Waldenhausen, a heavy thundering trot was heard ringing from the frozen road, as of a regular body of cavalry advancing rapidly upon their encampment. There was no time to be lost; the officer instantly withdrew his yagers from the wood, posted a strong guard at the wood side, sounded the alarm throughout the camp, agreeably to the system of signals previously concerted, mounted about thirty men, whose horses and themselves were kept in perfect equipment during each of the night-watches, and then advancing to the head of the barriers, prepared to receive the party of strangers in whatever character they should happen to present themselves.

All this had been done with so much promptitude and decision, that, on reaching the barriers, the officer found the strangers not yet come up. In fact, they had halted at a strong outpost about a quarter of a mile in advance of Waldenhausen; and though one or two patrollers came dropping in from by-roads on the forest-heath, who reported them as enemies, from the indistinct view they had caught of their equipments, it had already become doubtful from their movements whether they would really prove so.

Two of their party were now descried upon the road, and nearly close up with the gates of Waldenhausen; they were accompanied by several of the guard from the outpost; and, immediately on being hailed, they exclaimed, "Friends, and from Klosterheim!"

He who spoke was a young cavalier, magnificent alike in his person, dress, and style of his appointments. He was superbly mounted, wore the decorations of a major-general in the imperial service, and scarcely needed the explanations which he gave to exonerate himself from the suspicion of being a leader of robbers under Holkerstein. Fortunately enough, also, at a period when officers of the most distinguished merit were too often unfaithful to their engagements, or passed with so much levity from service to service as to justify an indiscriminate jealousy of all who were not in the public eye, it happened that the officer of the watch, formerly, when mounting guard at the imperial palace, had been familiar with the personal appearance of the cavalier, and could speak of his own knowledge to the favor which he had enjoyed at the emperor's court. After short explanations, therefore, he was admitted, and thankfully welcomed in the camp; and the officer of the guard departed to receive with honor the generous volunteers at the outpost.

Meantime, the alarm, which was general throughout the camp, had assembled all the women to one quarter, where a circle of carriages had been formed for their protection. In their centre, distinguished by her height and beauty, stood the Lady Paulina, dispensing assistance from her wardrobe to any who were suffering from cold under this sudden summons to night air, and animating others, who were more than usually depressed, by the aids of consolation and of cheerful prospects. She had just turned her face away from the passage by which this little sanctuary communicated with the rest of the camp, and was in the act of giving directions to one of her attendants, when suddenly a well-known voice fell upon her ear. It was the voice of the stranger cavalier, whose natural gallantry had prompted him immediately to relieve the alarm, which, unavoidably, he had himself created; in a few words, he was explaining to the assembled females of the camp in what character, and with how many companions, he had come. But a shriek from Paulina interrupted him. Involuntarily she held out her open arms, and involuntarily she exclaimed, "Dearest Maximilian!" On his part, the young cavalier, for a moment or two at first, was almost deprived of speech by astonishment and excess of pleasure. Bounding forward hardly conscious of those who surrounded them, with a rapture of faithful love he caught the noble young beauty into his arms,—a movement to which in the frank innocence of her heart, she made no resistance; folded her to his bosom, and impressed a fervent kiss upon her lips; whilst the only words that came to his own were, "Beloved Paulina! O, most beloved lady! what chance has brought you hither?"

CHAPTER IV

In those days of tragical confusion, and of sudden catastrophe, alike for better or for worse,—when the rendings asunder of domestic charities were often without an hour's warning, when reunions were as dramatic and as unexpected as any which are exhibited on the stage, and too often separations were eternal,—the circumstances of the times concurred with the spirit of manners to sanction a tone of frank expression to the stronger passions, which the reserve of modern habits would not entirely license. And hence, not less than from the noble ingenuousness of their natures, the martial young cavalier, and the superb young beauty of the imperial house, on recovering themselves from their first transports, found no motives to any feeling of false shame, either in their own consciousness, or in the reproving looks of any who stood around them. On the contrary, as the grown-up spectators were almost exclusively female, to whom the evidences of faithful love are never other than a serious subject, or naturally associated with the ludicrous, many of them expressed their sympathy with the scene before them by tears, and all of them in some way or other. Even in this age of more fastidious manners, it is probable that the tender interchanges of affection between a young couple rejoining each other after deep calamities, and standing on the brink of fresh, perhaps endless separations, would meet with something of the same indulgence from the least interested witnesses.

Hence the news was diffused through the camp with

general satisfaction, that a noble and accomplished cavalier, the favored lover of their beloved young mistress, had joined them from Klosterheim, with a chosen band of volunteers, upon whose fidelity in action they might entirely depend. Some vague account floated about, at the same time, of the marauding attack upon the Lady Paulina's carriage. But naturally enough, from the confusion and hurry incident to a nocturnal disturbance, the circumstances were mixed up with the arrival of Maximilian, in a way which ascribed to him the merit of having repelled an attack, which might else have proved fatal to the lady of his heart. And this romantic interposition of Providence on a young lady's behalf, through the agency of her lover, unexpected on her part, and unconscious on his, proved so equally gratifying to the passion for the marvellous and the interest in youthful love, that no other or truer version of the case could ever obtain a popular acceptance in the camp, or afterwards in Klosterheim. And had it been the express purpose of Maximilian to found a belief, for his own future benefit, of a providential sanction vouchsafed to his connection with the Lady Paulina, he could not, by the best-arranged contrivances, have more fully attained that end.

It was yet short of midnight by more than an hour; and therefore, on the suggestion of Maximilian, who reported the roads across the forest perfectly quiet, and alleged some arguments for quieting the general apprehension for this night, the travellers and troops retired to rest, as the best means of preparing them to face the trials of the two next days. It was judged requisite, however, to strengthen the night-guard very considerably and to relieve it at least every two hours. That the poor sentinel on the forest side of the encampment had been in some mysterious way trepanned upon his post, was now too clearly ascertained, for he was miss-

ing; and the character of the man, no less than the absence of all intelligible temptation to such an act, forbade the suspicion of his having deserted. On this
quarter, therefore, a file of select marksmen were
stationed, with directions instantly to pick off every
moving figure that showed itself within their range. Of
these men Maximilian himself took the command; and
by this means he obtained the opportunity, so enviable
to one long separated from his mistress, of occasionally
conversing with her, and of watching over her safety. In
one point he showed a distinguished control over his
inclinations; for, much as he had to tell her, and ardently as he longed for communicating with her on various subjects of common interest, he would not suffer
her to keep the window down for more than a minute or
two in so dreadful a state of the atmosphere. She, on her
part, exacted a promise from him that he would leave
his station at three o'clock in the morning. Meantime, as
on the one hand she felt touched by this proof of her
lover's solicitude for her safety, so, on the other, she was
less anxious on his account, from the knowledge she
had of his long habituation to the hardships of a camp,
with which, indeed, he had been familiar from his child-
ish days. Thus debarred from conversing with her
lover, and at the same time feeling the most absolute
confidence in his protection, she soon fell placidly
asleep. The foremost subject of her anxiety and sorrow
was now removed; her lover had been restored to her
hopes; and her dreams were no longer haunted with
horrors. Yet, at the same time, the turbulence of joy and
of hope fulfilled unexpectedly had substituted its own
disturbances; and her sleep was often interrupted. But,
as often as that happened, she had the delightful pleasure of seeing her lover's figure, with its martial equipments, and the drooping plumes of his yager barrette,
as he took his station at her carriage, traced out on the

ground in the bright glare of the flambeaux. She awoke, therefore, continually to the sense of restored happiness; and at length fell finally asleep, to wake no more until the morning trumpet, at the break of day, proclaimed the approaching preparations for the general movement of the camp.

Snow had fallen in the night. Towards four o'clock in the morning, amongst those who held that watch there had been a strong apprehension that it would fall heavily. But that state of the atmosphere had passed off; and it had not in fact fallen sufficiently to abate the cold, or much to retard their march. According to the usual custom of the camp, a general breakfast was prepared, at which all, without distinction, messed together—a sufficient homage being expressed to superior rank by resigning the upper part of every table to those who had any distinguished pretensions of that kind. On this occasion Paulina had the gratification of seeing the public respect offered in the most marked manner to her lover. He had retired about day break to take an hour's repose,—for she found, from her attendants, with mingled vexation and pleasure, that he had not fulfilled his promise of retiring at an earlier hour, in consequence of some renewed appearances of a suspicious kind in the woods. In his absence, she heard a resolution proposed and carried, amongst the whole body of veteran officers attached to the party, that the chief military command should be transferred to Maximilian, not merely as a distinguished favorite of the emperor, but also, and much more, as one of the most brilliant cavalry officers in the imperial service. This resolution was communicated to him on his taking the place reserved for him, at the head of the principal breakfast-table; and Paulina thought that he had never appeared more interesting, or truly worthy of admiration, than under that exhibition of courtesy and modest dignity with which he first earnestly declined the honor in favor of older officers, and then finally complied with what he found to be the sincere wish of the company, by frankly accepting it. Paulina had grown up amongst military men, and had been early trained to a sympathy with military merit,—the very court of the emperor had something of the complexion of a camp,—and the object of her own youthful choice was elevated in her eyes, if it were at all possible that he should be so, by this ratification of his claims on the part of those whom she looked up to as the most competent judges.

Before nine o'clock the van of the party was in motion; then, with a short interval, came all the carriages of every description, and the Papenheim dragoons as a rear-guard. About eleven the sun began to burst out, and illuminated, with the cheerful crimson of a frosty morning, those horizontal draperies of mist which had previously stifled his beams. The extremity of the cold was a good deal abated by this time, and Paulina, alighting from her carriage, mounted a led horse, which gave her the opportunity, so much wished for by them both, of conversing freely with Maximilian. For a long time the interest and animation of their reciprocal communications, and the magnitude of the events since they had parted, affecting either or both of them directly, or in the persons of their friends, had the natural effect of banishing any dejection which nearer and more pressing concerns would else have called forth. But, in the midst of this factitious animation, and the happiness which otherwise so undisguisedly possessed Maximilian at their unexpected reunion, it shocked Paulina to observe in her lover a degree of gravity almost amounting to sadness, which argued in a soldier of his gallantry some overpowering sense of danger. In fact, upon being pressed to say the worst, Maximilian frankly avowed that he was ill at ease with regard to their prospects when the hour of trial should arrive; and that hour he had no hope of evading. Holkerstein, he well knew, had been continually receiving reports of their condition, as they reached their nightly stations, for the last three days. Spies had been round about them, and even in the midst of them, throughout the darkness of the last night. Spies were keeping pace with them as they advanced. The certainty of being attacked was therefore pretty nearly absolute. Then, as to their means of defence, and the relations of strength between the parties, in numbers it was not impossible that Holkerstein might triple themselves. The *élite* of their own men might be superior to most of his, though counting amongst their number many deserters from veteran regiments; but the horses of their own party were in general poor and out of condition,—and of the whole train, whom Maximilian had inspected at starting, not two hundred could be pronounced fit for making or sustaining a charge. It was true that by mounting some of their picked troopers upon the superior horses of the most distinguished amongst the travellers, who had willingly consented to an arrangement of this nature for the general benefit, some partial remedy had been applied to their weakness in that one particular. But there were others in which Holkerstein had even greater advantages; more especially, the equipments of his partisans were entirely new, having been plundered from an ill-guarded armory near Munich, or from convoys which he had attacked. "Who would be a gentleman," says an old proverb, "let him storm a town;" and the gay appearance of this robber's companions threw a light upon its meaning. The ruffian companions of this marauder were, besides, animated by hopes such as no regular commander in an honorable service could find the means of holding out. And, finally, they were familiar with all the forest roads and innumerable bypaths, on which it was that the best points lay for surprising an enemy, or for a retreat; whilst, in their own case, encumbered with the protection of a large body of travellers and helpless people, whom, under any circumstances, it was hazardous to leave, they were tied up to the most slavish dependency upon the weakness of their companions; and had it not in their power either to evade the most evident advantages on the side of the enemy, or to pursue such as they might be fortunate enough to create for themselves.

"But, after all," said Maximilian, assuming a tone of gayety, upon finding that the candor of his explanations had depressed his fair companion, "the saying of an old Swedish enemy of mine is worth remembering in such cases,—that, nine times out of ten, a drachm of good luck is worth an ounce of good contrivance,—and were it not, dearest Paulina, that you are with us, I would think the risk not heavy. Perhaps, by to-morrow's sunset, we shall all look back from our pleasant seats in the warm refectories of Klosterheim, with something of scorn, upon our present apprehensions.—And see! at this very moment the turn of the road has brought us in view of our port, though distant from us, according to the windings of the forest, something more than twenty miles. That range of hills, which you observe ahead, but a little inclined to the left, overhangs Klosterheim; and, with the sun in a more favorable quarter, you might even at this point descry the pinnacles of the citadel, or the loftiest of the convent towers. Half an hour will bring us to the close of our day's march."

In reality, a few minutes sufficed to bring them within view of the *chateau* where their quarters had been prepared for this night. This was a great hunting establishment, kept up at vast expense by the two last and present Landgraves of X——. Many interesting anecdotes were connected with the history of this building; and the beauty of the forest scenery was conspicuous even in

winter, enlivened as the endless woods continued to be
by the scarlet berries of mountain-ash, or the dark ver-
dure of the holly and the ilex. Under her present frame
of pensive feeling, the quiet lawns and long-
withdrawing glades of these vast woods had a touching
effect upon the feelings of Paulina; their deep silence,
and the tranquillity which reigned amongst them, contrasting in her remembrance with the hideous scenes of
carnage and desolation through which her path had too
often lain. With these predisposing influences to aid
him, Maximilian found it easy to draw off her attention
from the dangers which pressed upon their situation.
Her sympathies were so quick with those whom she
loved, that she readily adopted their apparent hopes or
their fears; and so entire was her confidence in the
superior judgment and the perfect gallantry of her
lover, that her countenance reflected immediately the
prevailing expression of his.

Under these impressions Maximilian suffered her to
remain. It seemed cruel to disturb her with the truth.
He was sensible that continued anxiety, and dreadful or
afflicting spectacles, had with her, as with most persons
of her sex in Germany at that time, unless protected by
singular insensibility, somewhat impaired the firm tone
of her mind. He was determined, therefore, to consult
her comfort, by disguising or palliating their true situation. But, for his own part, he could not hide from his
conviction the extremity of their danger; nor could he,
when recurring to the precious interests at stake upon
the issue of that and the next day's trials, face with any
firmness the afflicting results to which they tended,
under the known barbarity and ruffian character of
their unprincipled enemy.

CHAPTER V

THE chateau of Falkenberg, which the travellers reached with the decline of light, had the usual dependences of offices and gardens, which may be supposed essential to a prince's hunting establishment in that period. It stood at a distance of eighteen miles from Klosterheim, and presented the sole *oasis* of culture and artificial beauty throughout the vast extent of those wild tracts of sylvan ground.

The great central pile of the building was dismantled of furniture; but the travellers carried with them, as was usual in the heat of war, all the means of fencing against the cold, and giving even a luxurious equipment to their dormitories. In so large a party, the deficiencies of one were compensated by the redundant contributions of another. And so long as they were not under the old Roman interdict, excluding them from seeking fire and water of those on whom their day's journey had thrown them, their own travelling stores enabled them to accommodate themselves to all other privations. On this occasion, however, they found more than they had expected; for there was at Falkenberg a store of all the game in season, constantly kept up for the use of the Landgrave's household, and the more favored monasteries at Klosterheim. The small establishment of keepers, foresters, and other servants, who occupied the chateau, had received no orders to refuse the hospitality usually practised in the Landgrave's name; or thought proper to dissemble them in their present circumstances of inability to resist. And having from necessity permitted so much, they were led by a sense of their master's honor, or their own sympathy with the condition of so many women and children, to do more. Rations of game were distributed liberally to all the messes; wine was not refused by the old *kellermeister*, who rightly considered that some thanks, and smiles of courteous acknowledgment, might be a better payment than the hard knocks with which military paymasters were sometimes apt to settle their accounts. And, upon the whole, it was agreed that no such evening of comfort, and even luxurious enjoyment, had been spent since their departure from Vienna.

One wing of the chateau was magnificently furnished. This, which of itself was tolerably extensive, had been resigned to the use of Paulina, Maximilian, and others of the military gentlemen, whose manners and deportment seemed to entitle them to superior attentions. Here, amongst many marks of refinement and intellectual culture, there was a library and a gallery of portraits. In the library some of the officers had detected sufficient evidences of the Swedish alliances clandestinely maintained by the Landgrave; numbers of rare books, bearing the arms of different imperial cities, which, in the several campaigns of Gustavus, had been appropriated as they fell in his hands, by way of fair reprisals for the robbery of the whole Palatine library at Heidelberg, had been since transferred (as it thus appeared) to the Landgrave, by purchase or as presents; and on either footing argued a correspondence with the emperor's enemies, which hitherto he had strenuously disavowed. The picture-gallery, it was very probable, had been collected in the same manner. It contained little else than portraits, but these were truly admirable and interesting, being all recent works from the pencil of Vandyke, and composing a series of heads and features the most remarkable for station in the one sex, or

for beauty in the other, which that age presented.
Amongst them were nearly all the imperial leaders of
distinction, and many of the Swedish. Maximilian and
his brother officers took the liveliest pleasure in peram-
bulating this gallery with Paulina, and reviewing with
her these fine historical memorials. Out of their joint
recollections, or the facts of their personal experience,
they were able to supply any defective links in that commentary which her own knowledge of the imperial
court would have enabled her in so many instances to
furnish upon this martial register of the age.

The wars of the Netherlands had transplanted to
Germany that stock upon which the camps of the Thirty
Years' War were originally raised. Accordingly, a
smaller gallery, at right angles with the great one, presented a series of portraits from the old Spanish leaders
and Walloon partisans. From Egmont and Horn, the
Duke of Alva and Parma, down to Spinola, the last of
that distinguished school of soldiers, no man of emi-
nence was omitted. Even the worthless and insolent Earl
of Leicester with his gallant nephew,—that *ultimus
Romanorum* in the rolls of chivalry,—were not excluded,
though it was pretty evident that a Catholic zeal had
presided in forming the collection. For, together with
the Prince of Orange, and *Henri Quatre,* were to be seen
their vile assassins—portrayed with a lavish ostentation
of ornament, and enshrined in a frame so gorgeous as
raised them in some degree to the rank of consecrated
martyrs.

From these past generations of eminent persons, who
retained only a traditional or legendary importance in
the eyes of most who were now reviewing them, all
turned back with delight to the active spirits of their
own day, many of them yet living, and as warm with life
and heroic aspirations as their inimitable portraits had
represented them. Here was Tilly, the "little corporal,"

now recently stretched in a soldier's grave, with his wily and inflexible features. Over against him was his great enemy, who had first taught him the hard lesson of retreating, Gustavus Adolphus, with his colossal bust, and "atlantéan shoulders, fit to bear the weight of mightiest monarchies." He also had perished, and too probably by the double crime of assassination and private treason; but the public glory of his short career was proclaimed in the ungenerous exultations of Catholic Rome from Vienna to Madrid, and the individual heroism in the lamentations of soldiers under every banner which now floated in Europe. Beyond him ran the long line of imperial generals,—from Wallenstein, the magnificent and the imaginative, with Hamlet's infirmity of purpose, De Mercy, etc., down to the heroes of partisan warfare, Holk, the Butlers, and the noble Papenheim, or nobler Piccolómini. Below them were ranged Gustavus Horn, Banier, the Prince of Saxe-Weimer, the Rhinegrave, and many other Protestant commanders, whose names and military merits were familiar to Paulina, though she now beheld their features for the first time. Maximilian was here the best interpreter that she could possibly have met with. For he had not only seen the greater part of them on the field of battle, but, as a favorite and confidential officer of the emperor's, had personally been concerned in diplomatic transactions with the most distinguished amongst them.

Midnight insensibly surprised them whilst pursuing the many interesting historical remembrances which the portraits called up. Most of the company, upon this warning of the advanced hour, began to drop off; some to rest, and some upon the summons of the military duty which awaited them in their turn. In this way, Maximilian and Paulina were gradually left alone, and now at length found a time which had not before offered for communicating freely all that pressed upon their hearts. Maximilian, on his part, going back to the period of their last sudden separation, explained his own sudden disappearance from Vienna. At a moment's warning, he had been sent off with sealed orders from the emperor, to be first opened in Klosterheim: the mission upon which he had been despatched was of consequence to the imperial interests, and through his majesty's favor would eventually prove so to his own. Thus it was that he had been peremptorily cut off from all opportunity of communicating to herself the purpose and direction of his journey previously to his departure from Vienna; and if his majesty had not taken that care upon himself, but had contented himself, in the most general terms, with assuring Paulina that Maximilian was absent on a private mission, doubtless his intention had been the kind one of procuring her a more signal surprise of pleasure upon his own sudden return. Unfortunately, however, that return had become impossible: things had latterly taken a turn which embarrassed himself, and continued to require his presence. These perplexities had been for some time known to the emperor; and, upon reflection, he doubted not that her own journey, undertaken before his majesty could be aware of the dangers which would beset its latter end, must in some way be connected with the remedy which the emperor designed for this difficult affair. But doubtless she herself was the bearer of sufficient explanations from the imperial ministers on that head. Finally, whilst assuring her that his own letters to herself had been as frequent as in any former absence, Maximilian confessed that he did not feel greatly astonished at the fact of none at all having reached her, when he recollected that to the usual adverse accidents of war, daily intercepting all messengers not powerfully escorted, were to be added, in this case, the express efforts of private malignity in command of all the forest passes.

This explanation recalled Paulina to a very painful sense of the critical importance which might be attached to the papers which she had lost. As yet, she had found no special opportunity, or, believing it of less importance, had neglected it, for communicating more than the general fact of a robbery. She now related the case more circumstantially, and both were struck with it, as at this moment a very heavy misfortune. Not only might her own perilous journey, and the whole purposes of the emperor embarked upon it, be thus rendered abortive; but their common enemies would by this time be possessed of the whole information which had been so critically lost to their own party, and perhaps would have it in their power to make use of themselves as instruments for defeating their own most important hopes.

Maximilian sighed as he reflected on the probability that a far shorter and bloodier event might defeat every earthly hope, within the next twenty-four hours. But he dissembled his feelings; recovered even a tone of gayety; and, begging of Paulina to dismiss this vexatious incident from her thoughts, as a matter that after all would probably be remedied by their first communication with the emperor, and before any evil had resulted from it, he accompanied her to the entrance of her own suite of chambers, and then returned to seek a few hours' repose for himself on one of the sofas he had observed in one of the small ante-rooms attached to the library.

The particular room which he selected for his purpose, on account of its small size, and its warm appearance in other respects, was furnished under foot with layers of heavy Turkey carpets, one laid upon another (according to a fashion then prevalent in Germany), and on the walls with tapestry. In this mode of hanging rooms, though sometimes heavy and sombre, there was a warmth sensible and apparent, as well as real, which peculiarly fitted it for winter apartments, and a massy splendor which accorded with the style of dress and furniture in that gorgeous age. One real disadvantage, however, it had as often employed; it gave a ready concealment to intruders with evil intentions; and under the protecting screen of tapestry many a secret had been discovered, many robberies facilitated, and some celebrated murderers had been sheltered with circumstances of mystery that forever baffled investigation.

Maximilian smiled as the sight of the hangings, with their rich colors glowing in the fire-light, brought back to his remembrance one of those tales which in the preceding winter had made a great noise in Vienna. With a soldier's carelessness, he thought lightly of all dangers that could arise within four walls; and having extinguished the lights which burned upon a table, and unbuckled his sabre, he threw himself upon a sofa which he drew near to the fire; and then enveloping himself in a large horseman's cloak, he courted the approach of sleep. The fatigues of the day, and of the preceding night, had made this in some measure needful to him. But weariness is not always the best preface to repose; and the irritation of many busy anxieties continued for some time to keep him in a most uneasy state of vigilance. As he lay, he could see on one side the fantastic figures in the fire composed of wood and turf; on the other side, looking to the tapestry, he saw the wild forms, and the *mêlée,* little less fantastic, of human and brute features in a chase—a boar-chase in front, and a stag-chase on his left hand. These, as they rose fitfully in bright masses of color and of savage expression under the lambent flashing of the fire, continued to excite his irritable state of feeling; and it was not for some time that he felt this uneasy condition give way to exhaustion. He was at length on the very point of falling asleep, or perhaps had already fallen into its very lightest and earliest stage, when the echo of a distant door awoke him. He had some slight impression that a noise in his own room had concurred with the other and more distant one to awake him. But, after raising himself for a moment on his elbow and listening, he again resigned himself to sleep.

Again, however, and probably before he had slept a minute, he was roused by a double disturbance. A low rustling was heard in some part of the room, and a heavy foot upon a neighboring staircase. Roused, at length, to the prudence of paying some attention to sounds so stealthy, in a situation beset with dangers, he rose and threw open the door. A corridor, which ran round the head of the staircase, was lit up with a brilliant light; and he could command from this station one flight of the stairs. On these he saw nothing; all was now wrapt in a soft effulgence of light, and in absolute silence. No sound recurring after a minute's attention, and indisposed by weariness to any stricter examination, where all examination from one so little acquainted with the localities might prove unavailing, he returned to his own room; but, before again lying down, he judged it prudent to probe the concealments of the tapestry by carrying his sabre round, and everywhere pressing the hangings to the wall. In this trial he met with no resistance at any point; and willingly believing that he had been deceived, or that his ear had exaggerated some trivial sound, in a state of imperfect slumber, he again laid down and addressed himself to sleep. Still there were remembrances which occurred at this moment to disturb him. The readiness with which they had been received at the chateau was in itself suspicious. He remembered the obstinate haunting of their camp on the preceding night, and the robbery conducted with so much knowledge of circumstances. Jonas Melk, the brutal landlord of Waldenhausen, a man known to him by repute (though not personally), as one of the vilest agents employed by the Landgrave, had been actively engaged in his master's service at their preceding stage. He was probably one of those who haunted the wood through the night. And he had been repeatedly informed through the course of the day that this man in particular, whose features were noticed by the yagers, on occasion of their officer's reproach to him, had been seen at intervals in company with others, keeping a road parallel to their own, and steadily watching their order of advance.

These recollections, now laid together, impressed him with some uneasiness. But overpowering weariness gave him a strong interest in dismissing them. And a soldier, with the images of fifty combats fresh in his mind, does not willingly admit the idea of danger from a single arm, and in a situation of household security. Pshaw! he exclaimed, with some disdain, as these martial remembrances rose up before him, especially as the silence had now continued undisturbed for a quarter of an hour. In five minutes more he had fallen profoundly asleep and, in less than one half-hour, as he afterwards judged, he was suddenly awakened by a dagger at his throat.

At one bound he sprung upon his feet. The cloak, in which he had been enveloped, caught upon some of the buckles or ornamented work of his appointments, and for a moment embarrassed his motions. There was no light, except what came from the sullen and intermitting gleams of the fire. But even this was sufficient to show him the dusky outline of two figures. With the foremost he grappled, and, raising him in his arms, threw him powerfully upon the floor, with a force that left him stunned and helpless. The other had endeavored to pinion his arms from behind; for the body-armor, which Maximilian had not laid aside for the

night, under the many anticipations of service which
their situation suggested, proved a sufficient protection
against the blows of the assassin's poniard. Impatient of
the darkness and uncertainty, Maximilian rushed to the
door and flung it violently open. The assassin still clung
to his arms, conscious that if he once forfeited his hold
until he had secured a retreat, he should be taken at
disadvantage. But Maximilian, now drawing a petronel
which hung at his belt, cocked it as rapidly as his embarrassed motions allowed him. The assassin faltered, conscious that a moment's relaxation of grasp would enable
his antagonist to turn the muzzle over his shoulder.
Maximilian, on the other hand, now perfectly awake,
and with the benefit of that self-possession which the
other so entirely wanted, felt the nervous tremor in the
villain's hands; and, profiting by this moment of indeci-
sion, made a desperate effort, released one arm, which
he used with so much effect as immediately to liberate
the other, and then intercepting the passage to the
stairs, wheeled round upon his murderous enemy, and,
presenting the petronel to his breast, bade him surrender his arms if he hoped for quarter.

The man was an athletic, and, obviously, a most powerful ruffian. On his face he carried more than one
large glazed cicatrix, that assisted the savage expression
of malignity impressed by nature upon his features.
And his matted black hair, with its elf locks, completed
the picturesque effect of a face that proclaimed, in every
lineament, a reckless abandonment to cruelty and ferocious passions. Maximilian himself, familiar as he was
with the faces of military butchers in the dreadful hours
of sack and carnage, recoiled for one instant from this
hideous ruffian, who had not even the palliations of
youth in his favor, for he seemed fifty at the least. All
this had passed in an instant of time; and now, as he
recovered himself from his momentary shock at so hate-

ful an expression of evil passions, great was Maximilian's astonishment to perceive his antagonist apparently speechless, and struggling with some over-mastering sense of horror, that convulsed his features, and for a moment glazed his eye.

Maximilian looked around for the object of his alarm; but in vain. In reality it was himself, in connection with some too dreadful remembrances, now suddenly awakened, that had thus overpowered the man's nerves. The brilliant light of a large chandelier, which overhung the staircase, fell strongly upon Maximilian's features; and the excitement of the moment gave to them the benefit of their fullest expression. Prostrate on the ground, and abandoning his dagger without an effort at retaining it, the man gazed, as if under a rattlesnake's fascination, at the young soldier before him. Suddenly he recovered his voice; and, with a piercing cry of unaffected terror, exclaimed, "Save me, save me, blessed Virgin! Prince, noble prince, forgive me! Will the grave not hold its own? Jesu Maria! who could have believed it?"

"Listen, fellow!" interrupted Maximilian. "What prince is it you speak of? For whom do you take me? speak truly, and abuse not my forbearance."

"Ha! and his own voice too! and here on this spot! God is just! Yet do thou, good patron, holy St. Ermengarde, deliver me from the avenger!"

"Man, you rave! Stand up, recover yourself, and answer me to what I shall ask thee: speak truly, and thou shalt have thy life. Whose gold was it that armed thy hand against one who had injured neither thee nor thine?"

But he spoke to one who could no longer hear. The man grovelled on the ground, and hid his face from a being, whom, in some incomprehensible way, he regarded as an apparition from the other world.

Multitudes of persons had by this time streamed in, summoned by the noise of the struggle from all parts of the chateau. Some fancied that, in the frenzied assassin on the ground, whose panic too manifestly attested itself as genuine, they recognized one of those who had so obstinately dogged them by side-paths in the forest. Whoever he was, and upon whatever mission employed, he was past all rational examination; at the aspect of Maximilian, he relapsed into convulsive horrors, which soon became too fit for medical treatment to allow of any useful judicial inquiry; and for the present he was consigned to the safe-keeping of the provost-marshal.

His companion, meantime, had profited by his opportunity, and the general confusion, to effect his escape. Nor was this difficult. Perhaps, in the consternation of the first moment, and the exclusive attention that settled upon the party in the corridor, he might even have mixed in the crowd. But this was not necessary. For, on raising the tapestry, a door was discovered which opened into a private passage, having a general communication with the rest of the rooms of that floor. Steps were now taken, by sentries disposed through the interior of the mansion, at proper points, to secure themselves from the enemies who lurked within, whom hitherto they had too much neglected for the avowed and more military assailants who menaced them from without. Security was thus restored. But a deep impression accompanied the party to their couches of the profound political motives, or (in the absence of those) of the rancorous personal malignity, which could prompt such obstinate persecution; by modes, also, and by hands, which encountered so many chances of failing; and which, even in the event of the very completest success for the present, could not be expected, under the eyes of so many witnesses, to escape a final exposure. Some enemy, of unusual ferocity, was too obviously working in the dark, and by agencies as mysterious as his own purpose.

Meantime, in the city of Klosterheim, the general interest in the fortunes of the approaching travellers had suffered no abatement, and some circumstances had occurred to increase the popular irritation. It was known that Maximilian had escaped with a strong party of friends from the city; but how, or by whose connivance, could in no way be discovered. This had drawn upon all persons who were known as active partisans against the Landgrave, or liable to suspicion as friends of Maximilian, a vexatious persecution from the military police of the town. Some had been arrested; many called upon to give security for their future behavior; and all had been threatened or treated with harshness. Hence, as well as from previous irritation and alarm on account of the party from Vienna, the whole town was in a state of extreme agitation.

Klosterheim, in the main features of its political distractions, reflected, almost as in a representative picture, the condition of many another German city. At that period, by very ancient ties of reciprocal service, strengthened by treaties, by religious faith, and by personal attachment to individuals of the imperial house, this ancient and sequestered city was inalienably bound to the interests of the emperor. Both the city and the university were Catholic. Princes of the imperial family, and Papal commissioners, who had secret motives for not appearing at Vienna, had more than once found a hospitable reception within the walls. And, amongst many acts of grace by which the emperors had acknowledged these services and marks of attachment, one of them had advanced a very large sum of money to the city chest for an indefinite time; receiving in return, as the warmest testimony of confidential gratitude which

the city could bestow, that *jus liberi ingressûs* which en-
titled the emperor's armies to a free passage at all times,
and, in case of extremity, to the right of keeping the city
gates and maintaining a garrison in the citadel. Unfortunately, Klosterheim was not *sui juris,* or on the roll of
free cities of the empire, but of the nature of an appanage in the family of the Landgrave of X——; and this
circumstance had produced a double perplexity in the
politics of the city; for the late Landgrave, who had been
assassinated in a very mysterious manner upon a hunting party, benefited to the fullest extent both by the
political and religious bias of the city—being a personal
friend of the emperor's, a Catholic, amiable in his deportment, and generally beloved by his subjects. But the
prince who had succeeded him in the Landgraviate, as
the next heir, was everywhere odious for the harshness
of his government, no less than for the gloomy austerity
of his character; and to Klosterheim in particular, which
had been pronounced by some of the first jurisprudents
a female appanage, he presented himself under the additional disadvantages of a very suspicious title, and a
Swedish bias too notorious to be disguised. At a time
when the religious and political attachments of Europe
were brought into collisions so strange, that the foremost auxiliary of the Protestant interest in Germany was
really the most distinguished cardinal in the church of
Rome, it did not appear inconsistent with this strong
leaning to the King of Sweden that the Landgrave was
privately known to be a Catholic bigot, who practised
the severest penances, and, tyrant as he showed himself
to all others, grovelled himself as an abject devotee at
the feet of a haughty confessor. Amongst the populace
of Klosterheim this feature of his character, confronted
with the daily proofs of his entire vassalage to the Swedish interest, passed for the purest hypocrisy; and he had
credit for no religion at all with the world at large. But

the fact was otherwise. Conscious from the first that he held even the Landgraviate by a slender title (for he was no more than cousin once removed to his immediate predecessor), and that his pretensions upon Klosterheim had separate and peculiar defects,—sinking of course with the failure of his claim as Landgrave, but not, therefore, prospering with its success,—he was aware that none but the most powerful arm could keep his princely cap upon his head. The competitors for any part of his possessions, one and all, had thrown themselves upon the emperor's protection. This, if no other reason, would have thrown him into the arms of Gustavus Adolphus; and with this, as it happened, other reasons of local importance had then and since cooperated. Time, as it advanced, brought increase of weight to all these motives. Rumors of a dark and ominous tendency, arising no one knew whence, nor by whom encouraged, pointed injuriously to the past history of the Landgrave, and to some dreadful exposures which were hanging over his head. A lady, at present in obscurity, was alluded to as the agent of redress to others, through her own heavy wrongs; and these rumors were the more acceptable to the people of Klosterheim, because they connected the impending punishment of the hated Landgrave with the restoration of the imperial connection; for, it was still insinuated, under every version of these mysterious reports, that the emperor was the ultimate supporter, in the last resort, of the lurking claims now on the point of coming forward to challenge public attention. Under these alarming notices, and fully aware that sooner or later he must be thrown into collision with the imperial court, the Landgrave had now for some time made up his mind to found a merit with the Swedish chancellor and general officers by precipitating an uncompromising rupture with his Catholic enemies, and thus to extract the grace of a voluntary act from what, in fact, he knew to be sooner or later inevitable.

Such was the positive and relative aspect of the several interests which were now struggling in Klosterheim. Desperate measures were contemplated by both parties; and, as opportunities should arise, and proper means should develop themselves, more than one party might be said to stand on the brink of great explosions. Conspiracies were moving in darkness, both in the council of the burghers and of the university. Imperfect notices of their schemes, and sometimes delusive or misleading notices, had reached the Landgrave. The city, the university, and the numerous convents, were crowded to excess with refugees. Malcontents of every denomination and every shade,—emissaries of all the factions which then agitated Germany; reformado soldiers, laid aside by their original employers, under new arrangements, or from private jealousies of new commanders; great persons with special reasons for courting a temporary seclusion, and preserving a strict incognito; misers, who fled with their hoards of gold and jewels to the city of refuge; desolate ladies, from the surrounding provinces, in search of protection for themselves, or for the honor of their daughters; and (not least distinguished among the many classes of fugitives) prophets and enthusiasts of every description, whom the magnitude of the political events, and their religious origin, so naturally called forth in swarms; these, and many more, in connection with their attendants, troops, students, and the terrified peasantry, from a circle of forty miles radius around the city as a centre, had swelled the city of Klosterheim, from a total of about seventeen, to six or seven and thirty thousand. War, with a slight reserve for the late robberies of Holkerstein, had as yet spared this favored nook of Germany. The great storm had whistled and raved around them; but hitherto none had

penetrated the sylvan sanctuary which on every side in-
vested this privileged city. The ground seemed charmed
by some secret spells, and consecrated from intrusion.
For the great tempest had often swept directly upon
them, and yet still had wheeled off, summoned away by
some momentary call, to some remoter attraction. But
now at length all things portended that, if the war
should revive in strength after this brief suspension, it
would fall with accumulated weight upon this yet un-
ravaged district.

This was the anticipation which had governed the
Landgrave's policy in so sternly and barbarously inter-
fering with the generous purposes of the Klosterheimers, for carrying over a safe-conduct to their friends and
visitors, when standing on the margin of the forest. The
robber Holkerstein, if not expressly countenanced by
the Swedes, and secretly nursed up to his present
strength by Richelieu, was at any rate embarked upon a
system of aggression which would probably terminate in
connecting him with one or other of those authentic
powers. In any case, he stood committed to a course of
continued offence upon the imperial interests; since in
that quarter his injuries and insults were already past
forgiveness. The interest of Holkerstein, then, ran in
the same channel with that of the Landgrave. It was
impolitic to weaken him. It was doubly impolitic to
weaken him by a measure which must also weaken the
Landgrave; for any deduction from his own military
force, or from the means of recruiting it, was in that
proportion a voluntary sacrifice of the weight he should
obtain with the Swedes on making the junction, which
he now firmly counted on, with their forces. But a result
which he still more dreaded from the cooperation of the
Klosterheimers with the caravan from Vienna, was the
probable overthrow of that supremacy in the city, which
even now was so nicely balanced in his favor that a slight

reinforcement to the other side would turn the scale against him.

In all these calculations of policy, and the cruel measures by which he supported them, he was guided by the counsels of Luigi Adorni, a subtle Italian, whom he had elevated from the post of a private secretary to that of sole minister for the conduct of state affairs. This man, who covered a temperament of terrific violence with a masque of Venetian dissimulation and the most icy reserve, met with no opposition, unless it were occasionally from Father Anselm, the confessor. He delighted in the refinements of intrigue, and in the most tortuous labyrinths of political manœuvring, purely for their own sakes; and sometimes defeated his own purposes by mere superfluity of diplomatic subtlety; which hardly, however, won a momentary concern from him, in the pleasure he experienced at having found an undeniable occasion for equal subtlety in unweaving his own webs of deception. He had been confounded by the evasion of Maximilian and his friends from the orders of the Landgrave; and the whole energy of his nature was bent to the discovery of the secret avenues which had opened the means to this elopement.

There were, in those days, as is well known to German antiquaries, few castles or fortresses of much importance in Germany, which did not communicate by subterraneous passages with the exterior country. In many instances these passages were of surprising extent, first emerging to the light in some secluded spot among rocks or woods, at the distance of two, three, or even four miles. There were cases even in which they were carried below the beds of rivers as broad and deep as the Rhine, the Elbe, or the Danube. Sometimes there were several of such communications on different faces of the fortress; and sometimes each of these branched, at some distance from the building, into separate arms, opening at intervals widely apart. And the uses of such secret communications with the world outside, and beyond a besieging enemy, in a land like Germany, with its prodigious subdivision of independent states and free cities, were far greater than they could have been in any one great continuous principality.

In many fortified places these passages had existed from the middle ages. In Klosterheim they had possibly as early an origin: but by this period it is very probable that the gradual accumulation of rubbish, through a course of centuries, would have unfitted them for use, had not the Peasants' War, in the time of Luther's reformation, little more than one hundred years before, given occasion for their use and repair. At that time Klosterheim had stood a siege, which, from the defect of artillery, was at no time formidable in a military sense; but as a blockade, formed suddenly when the citizens were slenderly furnished with provisions, it would certainly have succeeded, and delivered up the vast wealth of the convents as a spoil to the peasantry, had it not been for one in particular of these subterraneous passages, which, opening on the opposite side of the little river Iltiss, in a thick *boccage,* where the enemy had established no posts, furnished the means of introducing a continual supply of fresh provisions, to the great triumph of the garrison, and the utter dismay of the superstitious peasants, who looked upon the mysterious supply as a providential bounty to a consecrated cause.

So memorable a benefit had given to this one passage a publicity and an historical importance which made all its circumstances, and amongst those its internal mouth, familiar even to children. But this was evidently *not* the avenue by which Maximilian had escaped into the forest. For it opened externally on the wrong side of the river, whilst everybody knew that its domestic opening was in one of the chapels of the *schloss;* and another circumstance, equally decisive, was, that a long flight of stairs, by which it descended below the bed of the river, made it impassable to horses.

Every attempt, however, failed to trace out the mode of egress for the present. By his spies Adorni doubted not to find it soon; and, in the meantime, that as much as possible the attention of the public might be abstracted from the travellers and their concerns, a public proclamation was issued, forbidding all resort of crowds to the walls. These were everywhere dispersed on the ninth; and for that day were partially obeyed. But there was little chance that, with any fresh excitement to the popular interest, they would continue to command respect.

CHAPTER VI

THE morning of the tenth at length arrived—that day on which the expected travellers from Vienna, and all whom they had collected on their progress, ardently looked to rejoin their long-separated friends in Klosterheim, and by those friends were not less ardently looked for. On each side there were the same violent yearnings, on each side the same dismal and overpowering fears. Each party arose with palpitating hearts: the one looked out from Falkenberg with longing eyes, to discover the towers of Klosterheim; the other, from the upper windows or roofs of Klosterheim, seemed as if they could consume the distance between themselves and Falkenberg. But a little tract of forest ground was interposed between friends and friends, parents and children, lovers and their beloved. Not more than eighteen miles of shadowy woods, of lawns, and sylvan glades, divided hearts that would either have encountered death, or many deaths, for the other. These were regions of natural peace and tranquillity, that in any ordinary times should have been peopled by no worse inhabitants than the timid hare scudding homewards to its form, or the wild deer sweeping by with thunder to their distant lairs. But now from every glen or thicket armed marauders might be ready to start. Every gleam of sunshine in some seasons was reflected from the glittering arms of parties threading the intricacies of the thickets; and the sudden alarum of the trumpet rang oftentimes in the nights, and awoke the echoes that for centuries had been undisturbed, except by the hunter's horn in the most sequestered haunts of these vast woods.

Towards noon it became known, by signals that had been previously concerted between Maximilian and his college friends, that the party were advanced upon their road from Falkenberg, and, therefore, must of necessity on this day abide the final trial. As this news was dispersed abroad, the public anxiety rose to so feverish a point, that crowds rushed from every quarter to the walls, and it was not judged prudent to measure the civic strength against their enthusiasm. For an hour or two the nature of the ground and the woods forbade any view of the advancing party: but at length, some time before the light failed, the head of the column, and soon after the entire body, was descried surmounting a little hill, not more than eight miles distant. The black mass presented by mounted travellers and baggage-wagons was visible to piercing eyes; and the dullest could distinguish the glancing of arms, which at times flashed upwards from the more open parts of the forest.

Thus far, then, their friends had made their way without injury; and this point was judged to be within nine miles' distance. But in thirty or forty minutes, when they had come nearer by a mile and a half, the scene had somewhat changed. A heathy tract of ground, perhaps two miles in length, opened in the centre of the thickest woods, and formed a little island of clear ground, where all beside was tangled and crowded with impediments. Just as the travelling party began to deploy out of the woods upon this area at its further extremity, a considerable body of mounted troops emerged from the forest, which had hitherto concealed them, at the point nearest to Klosterheim. They made way rapidly; and in less than half a minute it became evident, by the motions of the opposite party, that they had been descried, and that hasty preparations were making for receiving them. A dusky mass, probably the black yagers, galloped up rapidly to the front and formed; after which it seemed to some eyes that the whole party again advanced, but still more slowly than before.

Every heart upon the walls of Klosterheim palpitated with emotion, as the two parties neared each other. Many almost feared to draw their breath, many writhed their persons in the anguish of rueful expectation, as they saw the moment approach when the two parties would shock together. At length it came; and, to the astonishment of the spectators, not more, perhaps, than of the travellers themselves, the whole cavalcade of strangers swept by, without halting for so much as a passing salute or exchange of news.

The first cloud, then, which had menaced their friends, was passed off as suddenly as it had gathered. But this, by some people, was thought to bear no favorable construction. To ride past a band of travellers from remote parts on such uncourteous terms argued no friendly spirit; and many motives might be imagined perfectly consistent with hostile intentions for passing the travellers unassailed, and thus gaining the means of coming at any time upon their rear. Prudent persons shook their heads, and the issue of an affair anticipated with so much anxiety certainly did not diminish it.

It was now four o'clock: in an hour or less it would be dark; and, considering the peculiar difficulties of the ground on nearing the town, and the increasing exhaustion of the horses, it was not judged possible that a party of travellers, so unequal in their equipments, and amongst whom the weakest was now become a law for the motion of the quickest, could reach the gates of Klosterheim before nine o'clock.

Soon after this, and just before the daylight faded, the travellers reached the nearer end of the heath, and again entered the woods. The cold and the darkness were now becoming greater at every instant, and it might have been expected that the great mass of the spectators would leave their station; but such was the intensity of the public interest, that few quitted the walls except for the purpose of reinforcing their ability to stay and watch the progress of their friends. This could be done with even greater effect as the darkness deepened, for every second horseman carried a torch; and, as much perhaps by way of signal to their friends in Klosterheim, as for their own convenience, prodigious flambeaux were borne aloft on halberds. These rose to a height which surmounted all the lower bushes, and were visible in all parts of the woods,—even the smaller lights, in the leafless state of the trees at this season of the year, could be generally traced without difficulty; and composing a brilliant chain of glittering points, as it curved and humored the road amongst the labyrinths of the forest, would have produced a singularly striking effect to eyes at leisure to enjoy it.

In this way, for about three hours, the travellers continued to advance unmolested, and to be traced by their friends in Klosterheim. It was now considerably after

seven o'clock, and perhaps an hour, or, at most, an hour
and a half, would bring them to the city gates. All hearts
began to beat high with expectation, and hopes were
loudly and confidently expressed through every part of
the crowd that the danger might now be considered as
past. Suddenly, as if expressly to rebuke the too pre-
sumptuous confidence of those who were thus
thoughtlessly sanguine, the blare of a trumpet was
heard from a different quarter of the forest, and about
two miles to the right of the city. Every eye was fastened
eagerly upon the spot from which the notes issued.
Probably the signal had proceeded from a small party in
advance of a greater; for in the same direction, but at a
much greater distance, perhaps not less than three miles
in the rear of the trumpet, a very large body of horse
was now descried coming on at a great pace upon the
line already indicated by the trumpet. The extent of the
column might be estimated by the long array of torches,
which were carried apparently by every fourth or fifth
man; and that they were horsemen was manifest from
the very rapid pace at which they advanced.

At this spectacle, a cry of consternation ran along the
whole walls of Klosterheim. Here, then, at last, were
coming the spoilers and butchers of their friends; for
the road upon which they were advancing issued at
right angles into that upon which the travellers, apparently unwarned of their danger, were moving. The
hideous scene of carnage would possibly pass immediately below their own eyes; for the point of junction between the two roads was directly commanded by
the eye from the city walls; and, upon computing the
apparent proportions of speed between the two parties,
it seemed likely enough that upon this very ground, the
best fitted of any that could have been selected, in a
scenical sense, as a stage for bringing a spectacle below
the eyes of Klosterheim, the most agitating of spectacles

would be exhibited,—friends and kinsmen engaged in mortal struggle with remorseless freebooters, under circumstances which denied to themselves any chance of offering assistance.

Exactly at this point of time arose a dense mist, which wrapped the whole forest in darkness, and withdrew from the eyes of the agitated Klosterheimers friends and foes alike. They continued, however, to occupy the walls, endeavoring to penetrate the veil which now concealed the fortunes of their travelling friends, by mere energy and intensity of attention. The mist, meantime, did not disperse, but rather continued to deepen; the two parties, however, gradually drew so much nearer, that some judgment could be at length formed of their motions and position, merely by the ear. From the stationary character of the sounds, and the continued recurrence of charges and retreats sounded upon the trumpet, it became evident that the travellers and the enemy had at length met, and too probable that they were engaged in a sanguinary combat. Anxiety had now reached its utmost height; and some were obliged to leave the walls, or were carried away by their friends, under the effects of overwrought sensibility.

Ten o'clock had now struck, and for some time the sounds had been growing sensibly weaker; and at last it was manifest that the two parties had separated, and that one, at least, was moving off from the scene of action; and, as the sounds grew feebler and feebler, there could be no doubt that it was the enemy, who was drawing off into the distance from the field of battle.

The enemy! ay, but how? Under what circumstances? As victor? Perhaps even as the captor of their friends! Or, if not, and he were really retreating as a fugitive and beaten foe, with what hideous sacrifices on the part of their friends might not that result have been purchased?

Long and dreary was the interval before these questions could be answered. Full three hours had elapsed since the last sound of a trumpet had been heard; it was now one o'clock, and as yet no trace of the travellers had been discovered in any quarter. The most hopeful began to despond; and general lamentations prevailed throughout Klosterheim.

Suddenly, however, a dull sound arose within a quarter of a mile from the city gate, as of some feeble attempt to blow a blast upon a trumpet. In five minutes more a louder blast was sounded close to the gate. Questions were joyfully put, and as joyfully answered. The usual precautions were rapidly gone through; and the officer of the watch being speedily satisfied as to the safety of the measure, the gates were thrown open, and the unfortunate travellers, exhausted by fatigue, hardships, and suffering of every description, were at length admitted into the bosom of a friendly town.

The spectacle was hideous which the long cavalcade exhibited as it wound up the steep streets which led to the market-place. Wagons fractured and splintered in every direction, upon which were stretched numbers of gallant soldiers, with wounds hastily dressed, from which blood had poured in streams upon their gay habiliments; horses, whose limbs had been mangled by the sabre; and coaches, or caleches, loaded with burthens of dead and dying; these were amongst the objects which occupied the van in the line of march, as the travellers defiled through Klosterheim. The vast variety of faces, dresses, implements of war, or ensigns of rank, thrown together in the confusion of night and retreat, illuminated at intervals by bright streams of light from torches or candles in the streets, or at the windows of the houses, composed a picture which resembled the chaos of a dream, rather than any ordinary spectacle of human life.

In the market-place the whole party were gradually assembled, and there it was intended that they should receive the billets for their several quarters. But such was the pressure of friends and relatives gathering from all directions, to salute and welcome the objects of their affectionate anxiety, or to inquire after their fate; so tumultuous was the conflict of grief and joy (and not seldom in the very same group), that for a long time no authority could control the violence of public feeling, or enforce the arrangements which had been adopted for the night. Nor was it even easy to learn, where the questions were put by so many voices at once, what had been the history of the night. It was at length, however, collected, that they had been met and attacked with great fury by Holkerstein, or a party acting under one of his lieutenants. Their own march had been so warily conducted after nightfall, that this attack did not find them unprepared. A barrier of coaches and wagons had been speedily formed in such an arrangement as to cripple the enemy's movements, and to neutralize great part of his superiority in the quality of his horses. The engagement, however, had been severe; and the enemy's attack, though many times baffled, had been as often renewed, until at length, the young general Maximilian, seeing that the affair tended to no apparent termination, that the bloodshed was great, and that the horses were beginning to knock up under the fatigue of such severe service, had brought up the very *élite* of his reserve, placed himself at their head, and, making a dash expressly at their leader, had the good fortune to cut him down. The desperateness of the charge, added to the loss of their leader, had intimidated the enemy, who now began to draw off, as from an enterprise which was likely to cost them more blood than a final success could have rewarded. Unfortunately, however, Maximilian, disabled by a severe wound, and entangled by his horse amongst the enemy, had been carried off a prisoner. In the course of the battle all their torches had been extinguished; and this circumstance, as much as the roughness of the road, the ruinous condition of their carriages and appointments, and their own exhaustion, had occasioned their long delay in reaching Klosterheim, after the battle was at an end. Signals they had not ventured to make; for they were naturally afraid of drawing upon their track any fresh party of marauders, by so open a warning of their course as the sound of a trumpet.

These explanations were rapidly dispersed through Klosterheim; party after party drew off to their quarters; and at length the agitated city was once again restored to peace. The Lady Paulina had been amongst the first to retire. She was met by the lady abbess of a principal convent in Klosterheim, to whose care she had been recommended by the emperor. The Landgrave also had furnished her with a guard of honor; but all expressions of respect, or even of kindness, seemed thrown away upon her, so wholly was she absorbed in grief for the capture of Maximilian, and in gloomy anticipations of his impending fate.

CHAPTER VII

THE city of Klosterheim was now abandoned to itself, and strictly shut up within its own walls. All roaming beyond those limits was now indeed forbidden even more effectually by the sword of the enemy than by the edicts of the Landgrave. War was manifestly gathering in its neighborhood. Little towns and castles within a range of seventy miles, on almost every side, were now daily occupied by imperial or Swedish troops. Not a week passed without some news of fresh military acces-

sions, or of skirmishes between parties of hostile for-
agers. Through the whole adjacent country, spite of the
severe weather, bodies of armed men were weaving to
and fro, fast as a weaver's shuttle. The forest rang with
alarums, and sometimes, under gleams of sunshine, the
leafless woods seemed on fire with the restless splendor
of spear and sword, morion and breast-plate, or the
glittering equipments of the imperial cavalry. Couriers,
or Bohemian gypsies, which latter were a class of people
at this time employed by all sides as spies or messengers,
continually stole in with secret despatches to the Landgrave, or (under the color of bringing public news, and
the reports of military movements) to execute some private mission for rich employers in town; sometimes
making even this clandestine business but a cover to
other purposes, too nearly connected with treason, or
reputed treason, to admit of any but oral communication.

What were the ulterior views in this large accumulation of military force, no man pretended to know. A
great battle, for various reasons, was not expected. But
changes were so sudden, and the counsels of each day so
often depended on the accidents of the morning, that
an entire campaign might easily be brought on, or the
whole burthen of war for years to come might be
transferred to this quarter of the land, without causing
any very great surprise. Meantime, enough was done
already to give a full foretaste of war and its miseries to
this sequestered nook, so long unvisited by that hideous
scourge.

In the forest, where the inhabitants were none, ex-
cepting those who lived upon the borders, and small
establishments of the Landgrave's servants at different
points, for executing the duties of the forest or the
chase, this change expressed itself chiefly by the tumultuous uproar of the wild deer, upon whom a murderous

war was kept up by the parties detached daily from
remote and opposite quarters, to collect provisions for
the half-starving garrisons, so recently, and with so little
previous preparation, multiplied on the forest skirts.
For, though the country had been yet unexhausted by
war, too large a proportion of the tracts adjacent to the
garrisons were in a wild, sylvan condition to afford any
continued supplies to so large and sudden an increase
of the population; more especially as, under the rumors
of this change, every walled town in a compass of a
hundred miles, many of them capable of resisting a sudden *coup-de-main* and resolutely closing their gates upon
either party, had already possessed themselves by purchase of all the surplus supplies which the country
yielded. In such a state of things, the wild deer became
an object of valuable consideration to all parties, and a
murderous war was made upon them from every side of
the forest. From the city walls they were seen in sweeping droves, flying before the Swedish cavalry for a
course of ten, fifteen, or even thirty miles, until headed
and compelled to turn by another party breaking suddenly from a covert, where they had been waiting their
approach. Sometimes it would happen that this second
party proved to be a body of imperialists, who were
carried by the ardor of the chase into the very centre of
their enemies before either was aware of any hostile
approach. Then, according to circumstances, came sudden flight or tumultuary skirmish; the woods rang with
the hasty summons of the trumpet; the deer reeled off
aslant from the furious shock, and, benefiting for the
moment by those fierce hostilities, originally the cause
of their persecution, fled far away from the scene of
strife; and not unfrequently came thundering beneath
the city walls, and reporting to the spectators above, by
their agitation and affrighted eyes, those tumultuous
disturbances in some remoter part of the forest, which

had already reached them in an imperfect way, by the interrupted and recurring echoes of the points of war—charges or retreats—sounded upon the trumpet.

But, whilst on the outside of her walls Klosterheim beheld even this unpopulous region all alive with military license and outrage, she suffered no violence from either party herself. This immunity she owed to her peculiar political situation. The emperor had motives for conciliating the city; the Swedes, for conciliating the Landgrave; indeed, they were supposed to have made a secret alliance with him, for purposes known only to the contracting parties. And the difference between the two patrons was simply this: that the emperor was sincere, and, if not disinterested, had an interest concurring with that of Klosterheim in the paternal protection which he offered; whereas the Swedes, in this, as in all their arrangements, regarding Germany as a foreign country, looked only to the final advantages of Sweden, or its German dependences, and to the weight which such alliances would procure them in a general pacification. And hence, in the war which both combined to make upon the forest, the one party professed to commit spoil upon the Landgrave, as distinguished from the city; whilst the Swedish allies of that prince prosecuted their ravages in the Landgrave's name, as essential to the support of his cause.

For the present, however, the Swedes were the preponderant party in the neighborhood; they had fortified the chateau of Falkenberg, and made it a very strong military post; at the same time, however, sending in to Klosterheim whatsoever was valuable amongst the furniture of that establishment, with a care which of itself proclaimed the footing upon which they were anxious to stand with the Landgrave.

Encouraged by the vicinity of his military friends that prince now began to take a harsher tone in Klosterheim.

The minor princes of Germany at that day were all ty-
rants in virtue of their privileges; and if in some rarer
cases they exercised these privileges in a forbearing
spirit, their subjects were well aware that they were indebted for this extraordinary indulgence to the temper
and gracious nature of the individual, not to the firm
protection of the laws. But the most reasonable and
mildest of the German princes had been little taught at
that day to brook opposition. And the Landgrave was by
nature, and the gloominess of his constitutional temperament, of all men the last to learn that lesson readily. He
had already met with just sufficient opposition from the
civic body and the university interest to excite his passion for revenge. Ample indemnification he determined
upon for his wounded pride; and he believed that the
time and circumstances were now matured for favoring
his most vindictive schemes. The Swedes were at hand,
and a slight struggle with the citizens would remove all
obstacles to their admission into the garrison; though,
for some private reasons, he wished to abstain from this
extremity, if it should prove possible. Maximilian also
was absent, and might never return. The rumor was
even that he was killed; and though the caution of
Adorni and the Landgrave led them to a hesitating re-
liance upon what might be a political fabrication of the
opposite party, yet at all events he was detained from
Klosterheim by some pressing necessity; and the period
of his absence, whether long or short, the Landgrave
resolved to improve in such a way as should make his
return unavailing.

Of Maximilian the Landgrave had no personal knowledge; he had not so much as seen him. But by his spies
and intelligencers he was well aware that he had been
the chief combiner and animater of the imperial party
against himself in the university, and by his presence
had given life and confidence to that party in the city

which did not expressly acknowledge him as their head. He was aware of the favor which Maximilian enjoyed with the emperor, and knew in general, from public report, the brilliancy of those military services on which it had been built. That he was likely to prove a formidable opponent, had he continued in Klosterheim, the Landgrave knew too well; and upon the advantage over him which he had now gained, though otherwise it should prove only a temporary one, he determined to found a permanent obstacle to the emperor's views. As a preliminary step, he prepared to crush all opposition in Klosterheim; a purpose which was equally important to his vengeance and his policy.

This system he opened with a series of tyrannical regulations, some of which gave the more offence that they seemed wholly capricious and insulting. The students were confined to their college bounds, except at stated intervals; were subject to a military muster, or calling over of names, every evening; were required to receive sentinels within the extensive courts of their own college, and at length a small court of guard; with numerous other occasional marks, as opportunities offered, of princely discountenance and anger.

In the university, at that time, from local causes, many young men of rank and family were collected. Those even who had taken no previous part in the cause of the Klosterheimers were now roused to a sense of personal indignity. And as soon as the light was departed, a large body of them collected at the rooms of Count St. Aldenheim, whose rank promised a suitable countenance to their purpose, whilst his youth seemed a pledge for the requisite activity.

The count was a younger brother of the Palsgrave of Birkenfeld, and maintained a sumptuous establishment in Klosterheim. Whilst the state of the forest had allowed of hunting, hawking, or other amusements, no man had exhibited so fine a stud of horses. No man had so large a train of servants; no man entertained his friends with such magnificent hospitalities. His generosity, his splendor, his fine person, and the courtesy with which he relieved the humblest people from the oppression of his rank, had given him a popularity amongst the students. His courage had been tried in battle: but, after all, it was doubted whether he were not of too luxurious a turn to undertake any cause which called for much exertion; for the death of a rich abbess, who had left the whole of an immense fortune to the count, as her favorite nephew, had given him another motive for cultivating peaceful pursuits, to which few men were, constitutionally, better disposed.

It was the time of day when the count was sure to be found at home with a joyous party of friends. Magnificent chandeliers shed light upon a table furnished with every description of costly wines produced in Europe. According to the custom of the times, these were drunk in cups of silver or gold, and an opportunity was thus gained, which St. Aldenheim had not lost, of making a magnificent display of luxury without ostentation. The ruby wine glittered in the jewelled goblet which the count had raised to his lips, at the very moment when the students entered.

"Welcome, friends," said the Count St. Aldenheim, putting down his cup, "welcome always; but never more than at this hour, when wine and good fellowship teach us to know the value of our youth."

"Thanks, count, from all of us. But the fellowship we seek at present must be of another temper; our errand is of business."

"Then, friends, it shall rest until to-morrow. Not for the Papacy, to which my good aunt would have raised a ladder for me of three steps,—Abbot, Bishop, Cardinal,—would I renounce the Tokay of to-night for the business of to-morrow. Come, gentlemen, let us drink my aunt's health."

"Memory, you would say, count."

"Memory, most learned friend,—you are right. Ah! gentlemen, she was a woman worthy to be had in remembrance: for she invented a capital plaster for gun-shot wounds; and a jollier old fellow over a bottle of Tokay there is not at this day in Suabia, or in the Swedish camp. And that reminds me to ask, gentlemen, have any of you heard that Gustavus Horn is expected at Falkenberg? Such news is astir; and be sure of this—that, in such a case, we have cracked crowns to look for. I know the man. And many a hard night's watching he has cost me; for which, if you please, gentlemen, we will drink his health."

"But our business, dear count—"

"Shall wait, please God, until to-morrow; for this is the time when man and beast repose."

"And truly, count, we are like—as you take things—to be numbered with the last. Fie, Count St. Aldenheim! are you the man that would have us suffer those things tamely which the Landgrave has begun?"

"And what now hath his serenity been doing? Doth he meditate to abolish Burgundy? If so, my faith! but we are, as you observe, little above the brutes. Or, peradventure, will he forbid laughing,—his highness being little that way given himself?"

"Count St. Aldenheim! it pleases you to jest. But we are assured that you know as well as we, and relish no better, the insults which the Landgrave is heaping upon us all. For example, the sentinel at your own door—doubtless you marked him? How liked you him?—"

"Methought he looked cold and blue. So I sent him a goblet of Johannisberg."

"You did? and the little court of guard—you have seen *that*? and Colonel von Aremberg, how think you of him?"

"Why surely now he's a handsome man: pity he wears so fiery a scarf! Shall we drink his health, gentlemen?"

"Health to the great fiend first!"

"As you please, gentlemen: it is for you to regulate the precedency. But at least,

> Here's to my aunt—the jolly old sinner,
> That fasted each day, from breakfast to dinner!
> Saw any man yet such an orthodox fellow,
> In the morning when sober, in the evening when
>   mellow?
>   Saw any man yet," &c.

"Count, farewell!" interrupted the leader of the party; and all turned round indignantly to leave the room.

"Farewell, gentlemen, as you positively will not drink my aunt's health; though, after all, she was a worthy fellow; and her plaster for gunshot wounds—"

But with that word the door closed upon the count's farewell words. Suddenly taking up a hat which lay upon the ground, he exclaimed, "Ah! behold! one of my friends has left his hat. Truly he may chance to want it on a frosty night." And, so saying, he hastily rushed after the party, whom he found already on the steps of the portico. Seizing the hand of the leader, he whispered,

"Friend! do you know me so little as to apprehend my jesting in a serious sense? Know that two of those whom you saw on my right hand are spies of the Landgrave. Their visit to me, I question not, was purposely made to catch some such discoveries as you, my friends, would too surely have thrown in their way, but for my determined rattling. At this time, I must not stay. Come again after midnight—farewell."

And then, in a voice to reach his guests within, he shouted, "Gentlemen, my aunt, the abbot of In-

gelheim,—abbess, I would say,—held that her spurs
were for her heels, and her beaver for her head. Where-
upon, baron, I return you your hat."

Meantime, the two insidious intelligencers of the
Landgrave returned to the palace with discoveries, not
so ample as they were on the point of surprising, but
sufficient to earn thanks for themselves, and to guide
the counsels of their master.

CHAPTER VIII

THAT same night a full meeting of the most distinguished students was assembled at the mansion of
Count St. Aldenheim. Much stormy discussion arose
upon two points. First, upon the particular means by
which they were to pursue an end upon which all were
unanimous. Upon that, however, they were able for the
present to arrive at a preliminary arrangement with
sufficient harmony. This was to repair in a body, with
Count St. Aldenheim at their head, to the castle, and
there to demand an audience of the Landgrave, at
which a strong remonstrance was to be laid before his
highness, and their determination avowed to repel the
indignities thrust upon them, with their united forces.
On the second they were more at variance. It happened
that many of the persons present, and amongst them
Count St. Aldenheim, were friends of Maximilian. A
few, on the other hand, there were, who, either from
jealousy of his distinguished merit, hated him; or, as
good citizens of Klosterheim, and connected by old family ties with the interests of that town, were disposed to
charge Maximilian with ambitious views of private ag-
grandizement, at the expense of the city, grounded
upon the emperor's favor, or upon a supposed mar-

riage with some lady of the imperial house. For the story
of Paulina's and Maximilian's mutual attachment had
transpired through many of the travellers; but with
some circumstances of fiction. In defending Maximilian
upon those charges, his friends had betrayed a natural
warmth at the injustice offered to his character; and the
liveliness of the dispute on this point had nearly ended
in a way fatal to their unanimity on the immediate question at issue. Good sense, however, and indignation at
the Landgrave, finally brought them round again to
their first resolution; and they separated with the unanimous intention of meeting at noon on the following day,
for the purpose of carrying it into effect.

But their unanimity on this point was of little avail;
for at an early hour on the following morning every one
of those who had been present at the meeting was arrested by a file of soldiers, on a charge of conspiracy,
and marched off to one of the city prisons. The Count
St. Aldenheim was himself the sole exception; and this
was a distinction odious to his generous nature, as it
drew upon him a cloud of suspicion. He was sensible
that he would be supposed to owe his privilege to some
discovery or act of treachery, more or less, by which he
had merited the favor of the Landgrave. The fact was,
that in the indulgence shown to the count no motive had
influenced the Landgrave but a politic consideration of
the great favor and influence which the count's brother,
the Palsgrave, at this moment enjoyed in the camp of his
own Swedish allies. On this principle of policy, the
Landgrave contented himself with placing St. Aldenheim under a slight military confinement to his own
house, under the guard of a few sentinels posted in his
hall.

For *him*, therefore, under the powerful protection
which he enjoyed elsewhere, there was no great anxiety
entertained. But for the rest, many of whom had no

friends, or friends who did them the ill service of enemies, being in fact regarded as enemies by the Landgrave and his council, serious fears were entertained by
the whole city. Their situation was evidently critical.
The Landgrave had them in his power. He was notoriously a man of gloomy and malignant passions; had
been educated, as all European princes then were, in
the notions of a plenary and despotic right over the lives
of his subjects, in any case where they lifted their pre-
sumptuous thoughts to the height of controlling the
sovereign; and, even in circumstances which to his own
judgment might seem to confer much less discretionary
power over the rights of prisoners, he had been suspected of directing the course of law and of punishment
into channels that would not brook the public knowledge. Darker dealings were imputed to him in the
popular opinion. Gloomy suspicions were muttered at
the fireside, which no man dared openly to avow; and in
the present instance the conduct of the Landgrave was
every way fitted to fall in with the worst of the public
fears. At one time he talked of bringing his prisoners to
a trial; at another, he countermanded the preparations
which he had made with that view. Sometimes he spoke
of banishing them in a body; and again he avowed his
intention to deal with their crime as treason. The result
of this moody and capricious tyranny was to inspire the
most vague and gloomy apprehensions into the minds
of the prisoners, and to keep their friends, with the
whole city of Klosterheim, in a feverish state of insecurity.

This state of things lasted for nearly three weeks; but
at length a morning of unexpected pleasure dawned
upon the city. The prisoners were in one night all released. In half an hour the news ran over the town and
the university; multitudes hastened to the college, anxious to congratulate the prisoners on their deliverance

from the double afflictions of a dungeon and of continual insecurity. Mere curiosity also prompted some, who took but little interest in the prisoners or their cause, to inquire into the circumstances of so abrupt and unexpected an act of grace. One principal court in the college was filled with those who had come upon this errand of friendly interest or curiosity. Nothing was to be seen but earnest and delighted faces, offering or acknowledging congratulation; nothing to be heard but the language of joy and pleasure—friendly or affectionate, according to the sex or relation of the speaker. Some were talking of procuring passports for leaving the town; some anticipating that this course would not be left to their own choice, but imposed, as the price of his clemency, by the Landgrave. All, in short, was hubbub and joyous uproar, when suddenly a file of the city guard, commanded by an officer, made their way rudely and violently through the crowd, advancing evidently to the spot where the liberated prisoners were collected in a group. At that moment the Count St. Aldenheim was offering his congratulations. The friends to whom he spoke were too confident in his honor and integrity to have felt even one moment's misgiving upon the true causes which had sheltered him from the Landgrave's wrath, and had thus given him a privilege so invidious in the eyes of those who knew him not, and on that account so hateful in his own. They knew his unimpeachable fidelity to the cause and themselves, and were anxiously expressing their sense of it by the warmth of their salutations at the very moment when the city guard appeared. The count, on his part, was gayly reminding them to come that evening and fulfil their engagement to drink his aunt of jovial memory in her own Johannisberg, when the guard, shouldering aside the crowd, advanced, and, surrounding the group of students, in an instant laid the hands of summary arrest each upon the gentleman who stood next him. The petty officer who commanded made a grasp at one of the most distinguished in dress, and seized rudely upon the gold chain depending from his neck. St. Aldenheim, who happened at the moment to be in conversation with this individual, stung with a sudden indignation at the ruffian eagerness of the men in thus abusing the privileges of their office, and unable to control the generous ardor of his nature, met this brutal outrage with a sudden blow at the officer's face, levelled with so true an aim, that it stretched him at his length upon the ground. No terrors of impending vengeance, had they been a thousand times stronger than they were, could at this moment have availed to stifle the cry of triumphant pleasure—long, loud, and unfaltering—which indignant sympathy with the oppressed extorted from the crowd. The pain and humiliation of the blow, exalted into a maddening intensity by this popular shout of exultation, quickened the officer's rage into an apparent frenzy. With white lips, and half suffocated with the sudden revulsion of passion, natural enough to one who had never before encountered even a momentary overture at opposition to the authority with which he was armed, and for the first time in his life found his own brutalities thrown back resolutely in his teeth, the man rose, and, by signs rather than the inarticulate sounds which he meant for words, pointed the violence of his party upon the Count St. Aldenheim. With halberds bristling around him, the gallant young nobleman was loudly summoned to surrender; but he protested indignantly, drawing his sword and placing himself in an attitude of defence, that he would die a thousand deaths sooner than surrender the sword of his father, the Palsgrave, a prince of the empire, of unspotted honor, and most ancient descent, into the hands of a jailer.

"Jailer!" exclaimed the officer, almost howling with passion.

"Why, then, captain of jailers, lieutenant, anspessade, or what you will. What else than a jailer is he that sits watch upon the prison-doors of honorable cavaliers?" Another shout of triumph applauded St. Aldenheim; for the men who discharged the duties of the city guard at that day, or "petty guard," as it was termed, corresponding in many of their functions to the modern police, were viewed with contempt by all parties; and most of all by the military, though in some respects assimilated to them by discipline and costume. They were industriously stigmatized as jailers; for which there was the more ground, as their duties did in reality associate them pretty often with the jailer; and in other respects they were a dissolute and ferocious body of men, gathered not out of the citizens, but many foreign deserters, or wretched runagates from the jail, or from the justice of the provost-marshal in some distant camp. Not a man, probably, but was liable to be reclaimed, in some or other quarter of Germany, as a capital delinquent. Sometimes, even, they were actually detected, claimed, and given up to the pursuit of justice, when it happened that the subjects of their criminal acts were weighty enough to sustain an energetic inquiry. Hence their reputation became worse than scandalous: the mingled infamy of their calling, and the houseless condition of wretchedness which had made it worth their acceptance, combined to overwhelm them with public scorn; and this public abhorrence, which at any rate awaited them, mere desperation led them too often to countenance and justify by their conduct.

"Captain of jailers! do your worst, I say," again ejaculated St. Aldenheim. Spite of his blinding passion, the officer hesitated to precipitate himself into a personal struggle with the count, and thus, perhaps, afford his antagonist an occasion for a further triumph. But loudly and fiercely he urged on his followers to attack him. These again, not partaking in the personal wrath of their leader, even whilst pressing more and more closely upon St. Aldenheim, and calling upon him to surrender, scrupled to inflict a wound, or too marked an outrage, upon a cavalier whose rank was known to the whole city, and of late most advantageously known for his own interests, by the conspicuous immunity which it had procured him from the Landgrave. In vain did the commanding officer insist, in vain did the count defy; menaces from neither side availed to urge the guard into any outrage upon the person of one who might have it in his power to retaliate so severely upon themselves. They continued obstinately at a stand, simply preventing his escape, when suddenly the tread of horses' feet arose upon the ear, and through a long vista were discovered a body of cavalry from the castle coming up at a charging pace to the main entrance of the college. Without pulling up on the outside, as hitherto they had always done, they expressed sufficiently the altered tone of the Landgrave's feelings towards the old chartered interests of Klosterheim, by plunging through the great archway of the college-gates; and then making way at the same furious pace through the assembled crowds, who broke rapidly away to the right and to the left, they reined up directly abreast of the city guard and their prisoners.

"Colonel von Aremberg!" said St. Aldenheim, "I perceive your errand. To a soldier I surrender myself; to this tyrant of dungeons, who has betrayed more men, and cheated more gibbets of their due, than ever he said *aves*, I will never lend an ear, though he should bear the orders of every Landgrave in Germany."

"You do well," replied the colonel; "but for this man, count, he bears no orders from any Landgrave, nor will ever again bear orders from the Landgrave of X——. Gentlemen, you are all my prisoners; and you will ac-

company me to the castle. Count St. Aldenheim, I am
sorry that there is no longer an exemption for yourself.
Please to advance. If it will be any gratification to you,
these men" (pointing to the city guard) "are prisoners
also."

Here was a revolution of fortune that confounded
everybody. The detested guardians of the city jail were
themselves to tenant it; or, by a worse fate still, were to
be consigned unpitied, and their case unjudged, to the
dark and pestilent dungeons which lay below the Landgrave's castle. A few scattered cries of triumph were
heard from the crowd; but they were drowned in a
tumult of conflicting feelings. As human creatures, fallen under the displeasure of a despot with a judicial
power of torture to enforce his investigations, even *they*
claimed some compassion. But there arose, to call off
attention from these less dignified objects of the public
interest, a long train of gallant cavaliers, restored so
capriciously to liberty, in order, as it seemed, to give the
greater poignancy and bitterness to the instant renewal
of their captivity. This was the very frenzy of despotism
in its very moodiest state of excitement. Many began to
think the Landgrave mad. If so, what a dreadful fate
might be anticipated for the sons or representatives of
so many noble families, gallant soldiers the greater part
of them, with a nobleman of princely blood at their
head, lying under the displeasure of a gloomy and infuriated tyrant, with unlimited means of executing the
bloodiest suggestions of his vengeance. Then in what
way had the guardians of the jails come to be connected
with any even imaginary offence? Supposing the Landgrave insane, his agents were not so; Colonel von Aremberg was a man of shrewd and penetrating understanding; and this officer had clearly spoken in the tone of
one who, whilst announcing the sentence of another,
sympathizes entirely with the justice and necessity of its
harshness.

Something dropped from the miserable leader of the city guard, in his first confusion and attempt at self-defence, which rather increased than explained the mystery. "The Masque! The Masque!" This was the word which fell at intervals upon the ear of the listening crowd, as he sometimes directed his words in the way of apology and deprecation to Colonel von Aremberg, who did not vouchsafe to listen, or of occasional explanation and discussion, as it was partly kept up between himself and one of his nearest partners in the imputed transgression. Two or three there might be seen in the crowd, whose looks avowed some nearer acquaintance with this mysterious allusion than it would have been safe to acknowledge. But, for the great body of spectators who accompanied the prisoners and their escort to the gates of the castle, it was pretty evident by their inquiring looks, and the fixed expression of wonder upon their features, that the whole affair, and its circumstances, were to them equally a subject of mystery for what was past, and of blind terror for what was to come.

CHAPTER IX

THE cavalcade, with its charge of prisoners, and its attendant train of spectators, halted at the gates of the *schloss*. This vast and antique pile had now come to be surveyed with dismal and revolting feelings, as the abode of a sanguinary despot. The dungeons and labyrinths of its tortuous passages, its gloomy halls of audience, with the vast corridors which surmounted the innumerable flights of stairs—some noble, spacious, and in the Venetian taste, capable of admitting the march of an army—some spiral, steep, and so unusually narrow

as to exclude two persons walking abreast; these, together with the numerous chapels erected in it to different saints by devotees, male or female, in the families of
forgotten Landgraves through four centuries back;
and, finally, the tribunals, or *gericht-kammern,* for dispensing justice, criminal or civil, to the city and territorial dependencies of Klosterheim; all united to compose
a body of impressive images, hallowed by great historical remembrances, or traditional stories, that from infancy to age dwelt upon the feelings of the Klosterheimers. Terror and superstitious dread predominated,
undoubtedly, in the total impression but the gentle virtues exhibited by a series of princes who made this
their favorite residence, naturally enough terminated in
mellowing the sternness of such associations into a religious awe, not without its own peculiar attractions. But,
at present, under the harsh and repulsive character of
the reigning prince, everything took a new color from
his ungenial habits. The superstitious legend, which had
so immemorially peopled the *schloss* with spectral appar-
itions, now revived in its earliest strength. Never was
Germany more dedicated to superstition in every shape
than at this period. The wild, tumultuous times, and the
slight tenure upon which all men held their lives, naturally threw their thoughts much upon the other world;
and communications with that, or its burthen of secrets,
by every variety of agencies, ghosts, divination, natural
magic, palmistry, or astrology, found in every city of the
land more encouragement than ever.

It cannot, therefore, be surprising that the well-
known apparition of the White Lady (a legend which
affected Klosterheim through the fortunes of its Landgraves, no less than several other princely houses of
Germany, descended from the same original stock)
should about this time have been seen in the dusk of the
evening at some of the upper windows in the castle, and

once in a lofty gallery of the great chapel during the
vesper service. This lady, generally known by the name
of the White Lady Agnes, or *Lady Agnes of Weissemburg,*
is supposed to have lived in the thirteenth or fourteenth
century, and from that time, even to our own days, the
current belief is, that on the eve of any great crisis of
good or evil fortune impending over the three or four
illustrious houses of Germany which trace their origin
from her, she makes her appearance in some conspicuous apartment, great baronial hall or chapel, of their
several palaces, sweeping along in white robes, and a
voluminous train. Her appearance of late in the *schloss*
of Klosterheim, confidently believed by the great body
of the people, was hailed with secret pleasure, as
forerunning some great change in the Landgrave's family,—which was but another name for better days to
themselves, whilst of necessity it menaced some great
evil to the prince himself. Hope, therefore, was predominant in their prospects, and in the supernatural
intimations of coming changes;—yet awe and deep religious feeling mingled with their hope. Of chastisement
approaching to the Landgrave they felt assured. Some
dim religious judgment, like that which brooded over
the house of Œdipus, was now at hand,—that was the
universal impression. His gloomy asceticism of life
seemed to argue secret crimes: these were to be brought
to light; for these, and for his recent tyranny, prosperous as it had seemed for a moment, chastisements were
now impending; and something of the awe which belonged to a prince so marked out for doom and fatal
catastrophe seemed to attach itself to his mansion,
more especially as it was there only that the signs and
portents of the coming woe had revealed themselves in
the apparition of the White Lady.

Under this superstitious impression, many of the
spectators paused at the entrance of the castle, and lin-

gered in the portal, though presuming that the chamber
of justice, according to the frank old usage of Germany,
was still open to all comers. Of this notion they were
speedily disabused by the sudden retreat of the few who
had penetrated into the first ante-chamber. These persons were harshly repelled in a contumelious manner,
and read to the astonished citizens another lesson upon
the new arts of darkness and concealment with which
the Landgrave found it necessary to accompany his new
acts of tyranny.

Von Aremberg and his prisoners, thus left alone in
one of the ante-chambers, waited no long time before
they were summoned to the presence of the Landgrave.

After pacing along a number of corridors, all car-
peted so as to return no sound to their footsteps, they
arrived in a little hall, from which a door suddenly
opened, upon a noiseless signal exchanged with an
usher outside, and displayed before them a long gallery,
with a table and a few seats arranged at the further end.
Two gentlemen were seated at the table, anxiously examining papers; in one of whom it was easy to recognize
the wily glance of the Italian minister; the other was the
Landgrave.

This prince was now on the verge of fifty, strikingly
handsome in his features, and of imposing presence,
from the union of a fine person with manners unusually
dignified. No man understood better the art of restrain-
ing his least governable impulses of anger or malignity
within the decorums of his rank. And even his worst
passions, throwing a gloomy rather than terrific air
upon his features, served less to alarm and revolt, than
to impress the sense of secret distrust. Of late, indeed,
from the too evident indications of the public hatred,
his sallies of passion had become wilder and more ferocious, and his self-command less habitually conspicuous.
But, in general, a gravity of insidious courtesy disguised

from all but penetrating eyes the treacherous purpose
of his heart.

The Landgrave bowed to the Count St. Aldenheim,
and, pointing to a chair, begged him to understand that
he wished to do nothing inconsistent with his regard for
the Palsgrave his brother; and would be content with his
parole of honor to pursue no further any conspiracy
against himself, in which he might too thoughtlessly
have engaged, and with his retirement from the city of
Klosterheim.

The Count St. Aldenheim replied that he and all the
other cavaliers present, according to his belief, stood
upon the same footing: that they had harbored no
thought of conspiracy, unless that name could attach to
a purpose of open expostulation with his highness on
the outraged privileges of their corporation as a university; that he wished not for any distinction of treatment
in a case when all were equal offenders, or none at all;
and, finally, that he believed the sentence of exile from
Klosterheim would be cheerfully accepted by all or most
of those present.

Adorni, the minister, shook his head, and glanced
significantly at the Landgrave, during this answer. The
Landgrave coldly replied that if he could suppose the
count to speak sincerely, it was evident that he was little
aware to what length his companions, or some of them,
had pushed their plots. "Here are the proofs!" and he
pointed to the papers.

"And now, gentlemen," said he, turning to the students, "I marvel that you, being cavaliers of family, and
doubtless holding yourselves men of honor, should be-
guile these poor knaves into certain ruin, whilst yourselves could reap nothing but a brief mockery of the
authority which you could not hope to evade."

Thus called upon, the students and the city guard
told their tale; in which no contradictions could be de-

tected. The city prison was not particularly well secured against attacks from without. To prevent, therefore, any sudden attempt at a rescue, the guard kept watch by turns. One man watched two hours, traversing the different passages of the prison; and was then relieved. At three o'clock on the preceding night, pacing a winding lobby, brightly illuminated, the man who kept that watch was suddenly met by a person wearing a masque, and armed at all points. His surprise and consternation were great, and the more so as the steps of The Masque were soundless, though the floor was a stone one. The guard, but slightly prepared to meet an attack, would, however, have resisted or raised an alarm; but The Masque, instantly levelling a pistol at his head with one hand, with the other had thrown open the door of an empty cell, indicating to the man by signs that he must enter it. With this intimation he had necessarily complied; and The Masque had immediately turned the key upon him. Of what followed he knew nothing until aroused by his comrades setting him at liberty, after some time had been wasted in searching for him.

The students had a pretty uniform tale to report. A Masque, armed cap-a-pie, as described by the guard, had visited each of their cells in succession; had instructed them by signs to dress, and then, pointing to the door, by a series of directions all communicated in the same dumb show, had assembled them together, thrown open the prison door, and, pointing to their college, had motioned them thither. This motion they had seen no cause to disobey, presuming their dismissal to be according to the mode which best pleased his highness; and not ill-pleased at finding so peaceful a termination to a summons which at first, from its mysterious shape and the solemn hour of night, they had understood as tending to some more formidable issue.

It was observed that neither the Landgrave nor his

minister treated this report of so strange a transaction with the scorn which had been anticipated. Both listened attentively, and made minute inquiries as to every circumstance of the dress and appointments of the mysterious Masque. What was his height? By what road, or in what direction, had he disappeared? These questions answered, his highness and his minister consulted a few minutes together; and then, turning to Von Aremberg, bade him for the present dismiss the prisoners to their homes; an act of grace which seemed likely to do him service at the present crisis; but at the same time to take sufficient security for their reappearance. This done, the whole body were liberated.

CHAPTER X

ALL Klosterheim was confounded by the story of the mysterious Masque. For the story had been rapidly dispersed; and on the same day it was made known in another shape. A notice was affixed to the walls of several public places in these words:

"Landgrave, beware! henceforth not you, but I, govern in Klosterheim.

(Signed)   THE MASQUE."

And this was no empty threat. Very soon it became apparent that some mysterious agency was really at work to counteract the Landgrave's designs. Sentinels were carried off from solitary posts. Guards, even of a dozen men, were silently trepanned from their stations. By and by, other attacks were made, even more alarming, upon domestic security. Was there a burgomaster amongst the citizens who had made himself conspicu-

ously a tool of the Landgrave, or had opposed the imperial interest? He was carried off in the night-time from
his house, and probably from the city. At first this was
an easy task. Nobody apprehending any special danger
to himself, no special preparations were made to meet
it. But as it soon became apparent in what cause The
Masque was moving, every person who knew himself
obnoxious to attack, took means to face it. Guards were
multiplied; arms were repaired in every house; alarm-
bells were hung. For a time the danger seemed to diminish. The attacks were no longer so frequent. Still,
wherever they were attempted, they succeeded just as
before. It seemed, in fact, that all the precautions taken
had no other effect than to warn The Masque of his own
danger, and to place him more vigilantly on his guard.
Aware of new defences raising, it seemed that he waited
to see the course they would take; once master of that,
he was ready (as it appeared) to contend with them as
successfully as before.

Nothing could exceed the consternation of the city.
Those even who did not fall within the apparent rule
which governed the attacks of The Masque felt a sense
of indefinite terror hanging over them. Sleep was no
longer safe; the seclusion of a man's private hearth, the
secrecy of bed-rooms, was no longer a protection. Locks
gave way, bars fell, doors flew open, as if by magic,
before him. Arms seemed useless. In some instances a
party of as many as ten or a dozen persons had been
removed without rousing disturbance in the neighborhood. Nor was this the only circumstance of mystery.
Whither he could remove his victims was even more
incomprehensible than the means by which he succeeded. All was darkness and fear; and the whole city
was agitated with panic.

It began now to be suggested that a nightly guard
should be established, having fixed stations or points of

rendezvous, and at intervals parading the streets. This was cheerfully assented to; for after the first week of the mysterious attacks, it began to be observed that the imperial party were attacked indiscriminately with the Swedish. Many students publicly declared that they had been dogged through a street or two by an armed Masque; others had been suddenly confronted by him in unfrequented parts of the city, in the dead of night, and were on the point of being attacked, when some alarm, or the approach of distant footsteps, had caused him to disappear. The students, indeed, more particularly, seemed objects of attack; and as they were pretty generally attached to the imperial interest, the motives of The Masque were no longer judged to be political. Hence it happened that the students came forward in a body, and volunteered as members of the nightly guard. Being young, military for the most part in their habits, and trained to support the hardships of night-watching, they seemed peculiarly fitted for the service; and, as the case was no longer of a nature to awaken the suspicions of the Landgrave, they were generally accepted and enrolled; and with the more readiness, as the known friends of that prince came forward at the same time.

A night-watch was thus established, which promised security to the city, and a respite from their mysterious alarms. It was distributed into eight or ten divisions, posted at different points, whilst a central one traversed the whole city at stated periods—and overlooked the local stations. Such an arrangement was wholly unknown at that time in every part of Germany, and was hailed with general applause.

To the astonishment, however, of everybody, it proved wholly ineffectual. Houses were entered as before; the college chambers proved no sanctuary; indeed, they were attacked with a peculiar obstinacy, which was understood to express a spirit of retaliation for the alacrity of the students in combining for the public protection. People were carried off as before. And continual notices affixed to the gates of the college, the convents, or the *schloss*, with the signature of *The Masque,* announced to the public his determination to persist, and his contempt of the measures organized against him.

The alarm of the citizens now became greater than ever. The danger was one which courage could not face, nor prudence make provision for, nor wiliness evade. All alike, who had once been marked out for attack, sooner or later fell victims to the obstinacy of this mysterious foe. To have received even an individual warning, availed them not at all. Sometimes it happened that, having received notice of suspicious circumstances indicating that The Masque had turned his attention upon themselves, they would assemble round their dwellings, or in their very chambers, a band of armed men sufficient to set the danger at defiance. But no sooner had they relaxed in these costly and troublesome arrangements, no sooner was the sense of peril lulled, and an opening made for their unrelenting enemy, than he glided in with his customary success; and in a morning or two after, it was announced to the city that they also were numbered with his victims.

Even yet it seemed that something remained in reserve to augment the terrors of the citizens, and push them to excess. Hitherto there had been no reason to think that any murderous violence had occurred in the mysterious rencontres between The Masque and his victims. But of late, in those houses, or college chambers, from which the occupiers had disappeared, traces of bloodshed were apparent in some instances, and of ferocious conflict in others. Sometimes a profusion of hair was scattered on the ground; sometimes fragments of dress, or splinters of weapons. Everything marked that on both sides, as this mysterious agency advanced, the passions increased in intensity; determination and murderous malignity on the one side, and the fury of resistance on the other.

At length the last consummation was given to the public panic; for, as if expressly to put an end to all doubts upon the spirit in which he conducted his warfare, in one house, where the bloodshed had been so great as to argue some considerable loss of life, a notice was left behind in the following terms: "Thus it is that I punish resistance; mercy to a cheerful submission; but henceforth death to the obstinate!—THE MASQUE."

What was to be done? Some counselled a public deprecation of his wrath, addressed to The Masque. But this, had it even offered any chance of succeeding, seemed too abject an act of abasement to become a large city. Under any circumstances, it was too humiliating a confession that, in a struggle with one man (for no more had avowedly appeared upon the scene), they were left defeated and at his mercy. A second party counselled a treaty; would it not be possible to learn the ultimate objects of The Masque; and, if such as seemed capable of being entertained with honor, to concede to him his demands, in exchange for security to the city, and immunity from future molestation? It was true that no man knew where to seek him: personally he was hidden from their reach; but everybody knew how to find him: he was amongst them; in their very centre; and whatever they might address to him in a public notice would be sure of speedily reaching his eye.

After some deliberation, a summons was addressed to The Masque, and exposed on the college gates, demanding of him a declaration of his purposes, and the price which he expected for suspending them. The next day an answer appeared in the same situation, avowing the intention of The Masque to come forward with ample explanation of his motives at a proper crisis, till which, "more blood must flow in Klosterheim."

CHAPTER XI

MEANTIME the Landgrave was himself perplexed and alarmed. Hitherto he had believed himself possessed of all the intrigues, plots, or conspiracies, which threatened his influence in the city. Among the students and among the citizens he had many spies, who communicated to him whatsoever they could learn, which was sometimes more than the truth, and sometimes a good deal less. But now he was met by a terrific antagonist, who moved in darkness, careless of his power, inaccessible to his threats, and apparently as reckless as himself of the quality of his means.

Adorni, with all his Venetian subtlety, was now as much at fault as everybody else. In vain had they deliberated together, day after day, upon his probable purposes; in vain had they schemed to intercept his person, or offered high rewards for tracing his retreats. Snares had been laid for him in vain; every wile had proved abortive, every plot had been counterplotted. And both involuntarily confessed that they had now met with their master.

Vexed and confounded, fears for the future struggling with mortification for the past, the Landgrave was sitting, late at night, in the long gallery where he usually held his councils. He was reflecting with anxiety on the peculiarly unpropitious moment at which his new enemy had come upon the stage; the very crisis of the struggle between the Swedish and imperial interest in Klosterheim, which would ultimately determine his own place and value in the estimate of his new allies. He was not of a character to be easily duped by mystery. Yet he could not but acknowledge to himself that there was something calculated to impress awe, and the sort of fear which is connected with the supernatural, in the sudden appearances, and vanishings as sudden, of The Masque. He came, no one could guess whence; retreated, no one could guess whither; was intercepted, and yet eluded arrest; and if half the stories in circulation could be credited, seemed inaudible in his steps, at pleasure to make himself invisible and impalpable to the very hands stretched out to detain him. Much of this, no doubt, was wilful exaggeration, or the fictions of fears self-deluded. But enough remained, after every allowance, to justify an extraordinary interest in so singular a being; and the Landgrave could not avoid wishing that chance might offer an opportunity to himself of observing him.

Profound silence had for some time reigned throughout the castle. A clock which stood in the room broke it for a moment by striking the quarters; and, raising his eyes, the Landgrave perceived that it was past two. He rose to retire for the night, and stood for a moment musing with one hand resting upon the table. A momentary feeling of awe came across him, as his eyes travelled through the gloom at the lower end of the room, on the sudden thought, that a being so mysterious, and capable of piercing through so many impediments to the interior of every mansion in Klosterheim, was doubtless likely enough to visit the castle; nay, it would be no ways improbable that he should penetrate to this very room. What bars had yet been found sufficient to repel him? And who could pretend to calculate the hour of his visit? This night even might be the time which he would select. Thinking thus, the Landgrave was suddenly aware of a dusky figure entering the room by a door at the lower end. The room had the

length and general proportions of a gallery, and the
further end was so remote from the candles which stood
on the Landgrave's table, that the deep gloom was but
slightly penetrated by their rays. Light, however, there
was, sufficient to display the outline of a figure slowly
and inaudibly advancing up the room. It could not be
said that the figure advanced stealthily; on the contrary,
its motion, carriage, and bearing, were in the highest
degree dignified and solemn. But the feeling of a
stealthy purpose was suggested by the perfect silence of
its tread. The motion of a shadow could not be more
noiseless. And this circumstance confirmed the Landgrave's first impression, that now he was on the point of
accomplishing his recent wish, and meeting that mysterious being who was the object of so much awe, and the
author of so far-spread a panic.

He was right; it was indeed The Masque, armed cap-
a-pie as usual. He advanced with an equable and determined step in the direction of the Landgrave. Whether
he saw his highness, who stood a little in the shade of a
large cabinet, could not be known; the Landgrave
doubted not that he did. He was a prince of firm nerves
by constitution, and of great intrepidity; yet, as one who
shared in the superstitions of his age, he could not be
expected entirely to suppress an emotion of indefinite
apprehension as he now beheld the solemn approach of
a being, who, by some unaccountable means, had
trepanned so many different individuals from so many
different houses, most of them prepared for self-
defence, and fenced in by the protection of stone walls,
locks, and bars.

The Landgrave, however, lost none of his presence of
mind; and, in the midst of his discomposure, as his eye
fell upon the habiliments of this mysterious person, and
the arms and military accoutrements which he bore,
naturally his thoughts settled upon the more earthly

means of annoyance which this martial apparition carried about him. The Landgrave was himself unarmed; he had no arms even within reach, nor was it possible for him in his present situation very speedily to summon assistance. With these thoughts passing rapidly through his mind, and sensible that, in any view of his nature and powers, the being now in his presence was a very formidable antagonist, the Landgrave could not but feel relieved from a burden of anxious tremors, when he saw The Masque suddenly turn towards a door which opened about half-way up the room, and led into a picture-gallery at right angles with the room in which they both were.

Into the picture-gallery The Masque passed at the same solemn pace, without apparently looking at the Landgrave. This movement seemed to argue, either that he purposely declined an interview with the prince,—and *that* might argue fear,—or that he had not been aware of his presence. Either supposition, as implying something of human infirmity, seemed incompatible with supernatural faculties. Partly upon this consideration, and partly, perhaps, because he suddenly recollected that the road taken by The Masque would lead him directly past the apartments of the old seneschal, where assistance might be summoned, the Landgrave found his spirits at this moment revive. The consciousness of rank and birth also came to his aid, and that sort of disdain of the aggressor, which possesses every man, brave or cowardly alike, within the walls of his own dwelling. Unarmed as he was, he determined to pursue, and perhaps to speak.

The restraints of high breeding, and the ceremonious decorum of his rank, involuntarily checked the Landgrave from pursuing with a hurried pace. He advanced with his habitual gravity of step, so that The Masque was half-way down the gallery before the prince entered it.

This gallery, furnished on each side with pictures, of which some were portraits, was of great length. The Masque and the prince continued to advance, preserving a pretty equal distance. It did not appear by any sign or gesture that The Masque was aware of the Landgrave's pursuit. Suddenly, however, he paused, drew his sword, halted; the Landgrave also halted; then, turning half round, and waving with his hand to the prince so as to solicit his attention, slowly The Masque elevated the point of his sword to the level of a picture—it was the portrait of a young cavalier in a hunting-dress, blooming with youth and youthful energy. The Landgrave turned pale, trembled, and was ruefully agitated. The Masque kept his sword in its position for half a minute; then dropping it, shook his head, and raised his hand with a peculiar solemnity of expression. The Landgrave recovered himself, his features swelled with passion, he quickened his step, and again followed in pursuit.

The Masque, however, had by this time turned out of the gallery into a passage, which, after a single curve, terminated in the private room of the seneschal. Believing that his ignorance of the localities was thus leading him on to certain capture, the Landgrave pursued more leisurely. The passage was dimly lighted; every image floated in a cloudy obscurity; and, upon reaching the curve, it seemed to the Landgrave that The Masque was just on the point of entering the seneschal's room. No other door was heard to open; and he felt assured that he had seen the lofty figure of The Masque gliding into that apartment. He again quickened his steps; a light burned within, the door stood ajar; quietly the prince pushed it open, and entered with the fullest assurance that he should here at length overtake the object of his pursuit.

Great was his consternation upon finding in a room, which presented no outlet, not a living creature except

the elderly seneschal, who lay quietly sleeping in his
arm-chair. The first impulse of the prince was to
awaken him roughly, that he might summon aid and
cooperate in the search. One glance at a paper upon the
table arrested his hand. He saw a name written there,
interesting to his fears beyond all others in the world.
His eye was riveted as by fascination to the paper. He
read one instant. That satisfied him that the old seneschal must be overcome by no counterfeit slumbers,
when he could thus surrender a secret of capital importance to the gaze of that eye from which, above all
others, he must desire to screen it. One moment he
deliberated with himself; the old man stirred, and muttered in his dreams; the Landgrave seized the paper,
and stood irresolute for an instant whether to await his
wakening, and authoritatively to claim what so nearly
concerned his own interest, or to retreat with it from the
room before the old man should be aware of the
prince's visit, or his own loss.

But the seneschal, wearied perhaps with some unusual exertion, had but moved in his chair; again he
composed himself to deep slumber, made deeper by the
warmth of a hot fire. The raving of the wind, as it
whistled round this angle of the *schloss*, drowned all
sounds that could have disturbed him. The Landgrave
secreted the paper; nor did any sense of his rank and
character interpose to check him in an act so unworthy
of an honorable cavalier. Whatever crimes he had
hitherto committed or authorized, this was, perhaps,
the first instance in which he had offended by an instance of petty knavery. He retired with the stealthy
pace of a robber, anxious to evade detection, and stole
back to his own apartments with an overpowering interest in the discovery he had made so accidentally, and
with an anxiety to investigate it further, which absorbed
for the time all other cares, and banished from his

thoughts even The Masque himself, whose sudden appearance and retreat had, in fact, thrown into his hands the secret which now so exclusively disturbed him.

CHAPTER XII

MEANTIME, The Masque continued to harass the Landgrave, to baffle many of his wiles, and to neutralize his most politic schemes. In one of the many placards which he affixed to the castle gates, he described the Landgrave as ruling in Klosterheim by day, and himself by night. Sarcasms such as these, together with the practical insults which The Masque continually offered to the Landgrave, by foiling his avowed designs, embittered the prince's existence. The injury done to his political schemes of ambition at this particular crisis was irreparable. One after one, all the agents and tools by whom he could hope to work upon the counsels of the Klosterheim authorities had been removed. Losing *their* influence, he had lost every prop of his own. Nor was this all; he was reproached by the general voice of the city as the original cause of a calamity which he had since shown himself impotent to redress. He it was, and his cause, which had drawn upon the people so fatally trepanned the hostility of the mysterious Masque. But for his highness, all the burgomasters, captains, city-officers, &c., would now be sleeping in their beds; whereas, the best fate which could be surmised for the most of them was, that they were sleeping in dungeons; some, perhaps in their graves. And thus the Landgrave's cause not merely lost its most efficient partisans, but, through their loss, determined the wavering against him, alienated the few who remained of his own faction, and gave strength and encouragement to the general dissatisfaction which had so long prevailed.

Thus it happened that the conspirators, or suspected conspirators, could not be brought to trial, or to punishment without a trial. Any spark of fresh irritation falling upon the present combustible temper of the populace, would not fail to produce an explosion. Fresh conspirators, and real ones, were thus encouraged to arise. The university, the city, teemed with plots. The government of the prince was exhausted with the growing labor of tracing and counteracting them. And, by little and little, matters came into such a condition, that the control of the city, though still continuing in the Landgrave's hands, was maintained by mere martial force, and at the very point of the sword. And, in no long time, it was feared, that with so general a principle of hatred to combine the populace, and so large a body of military students to head them, the balance of power, already approaching to an equipoise, would be turned against the Landgrave's government. And, in the best event, his highness could now look for nothing from their love. All might be reckoned for lost that could not be extorted by force.

This state of things had been brought about by the dreadful Masque, seconded, no doubt, by those whom he had emboldened and aroused within; and, as the climax and crowning injury of the whole, every day unfolded more and more the vast importance which Klosterheim would soon possess as the centre and key of the movements to be anticipated in the coming campaign. An electoral cap would perhaps reward the services of the Landgrave in the general pacification, if he could present himself at the German Diet as the possessor *de facto* of Klosterheim and her territorial dependences, and with some imperfect possession *de jure;* still more, if he could plead the merit of having brought over this state, so important from local situation, as a willing ally to the Swedish interest. But to this a free vote of the city was an essential preliminary; and from that, through the machinations of The Masque, he was now further than ever.

The temper of the prince began to give way under these accumulated provocations. An enemy forever aiming his blows with the deadliest effect; forever stabbing in the dark, yet charmed and consecrated from all retaliation; always met with, never to be found! The Landgrave ground his teeth, clenched his fists, with spasms of fury. He quarrelled with his ministers; swore at the officers; cursed the sentinels; and the story went through Klosterheim that he had kicked Adorni.

Certain it was, under whatever stimulus, that Adorni put forth much more zeal at last for the apprehension of The Masque. Come what would, he publicly avowed that six days more should not elapse without the arrest of this "ruler of Klosterheim by night." He had a scheme for the purpose, a plot baited for snaring him; and he pledged his reputation as a minister and an intriguer upon its entire success.

On the following day, invitations were issued by Adorni, in his highness' name, to a masqued ball on that day week. The fashion of masqued entertainments had been recently introduced from Italy into this sequestered nook of Germany; and here, as there, it had been abused to purposes of criminal intrigue.

Spite of the extreme unpopularity of the Landgrave with the low and middle classes of the city, among the highest his little court still continued to furnish a central resort to the rank and high blood converged in such unusual proportion within the walls of Klosterheim. The *schloss* was still looked to as the standard and final court of appeal in all matters of taste, elegance, and high breeding. Hence it naturally happened that everybody with any claims to such an honor was anxious to receive a ticket of admission;—it became the test for ascertaining a person's pretensions to mix in the first circles of society; and with this extraordinary zeal for obtaining an admission naturally increased the minister's rigor and fastidiousness in pressing the usual investigation of the claimant's qualifications. Much offence was given on both sides, and many sneers hazarded at the minister himself, whose pretensions were supposed to be of the lowest description. But the result was, that exactly twelve hundred cards were issued; these were regularly numbered, and below the device, engraved upon the card, was impressed a seal, bearing the arms and motto of the Landgraves of X—.

Every precaution was taken for carrying into effect the scheme, with all its details, as concerted by Adorni; and the third day of the following week was announced as the day of the expected *fête*.

CHAPTER XIII

THE morning of the important day at length arrived, and all Klosterheim was filled with expectation. Even those who were not amongst the invited shared in the anxiety; for a great scene was looked for, and perhaps some tragical explosion. The undertaking of Adorni was known; it had been published abroad that he was solemnly pledged to effect the arrest of The Masque; and by many it was believed that he would so far succeed, at the least, as to bring on a public collision with that extraordinary personage. As to the issue most people were doubtful, The Masque having hitherto so uniformly defeated the best-laid schemes for his apprehension. But it was hardly questioned that the public challenge offered to him by Adorni would succeed in bringing him before the public eye. This challenge had taken the shape of a public notice, posted up in the places where The Masque had usually affixed his own; and it was to the following effect: "That the noble strangers now in Klosterheim, and others invited to the Landgrave's *fête,* who might otherwise feel anxiety in presenting themselves at the *schloss,* from an apprehension of meeting with the criminal disturber of the public peace, known by the appellation of The Masque, were requested by authority to lay aside all apprehensions of that nature, as the most energetic measures had been adopted to prevent or chastise upon the spot any such insufferable intrusion; and for The Masque himself, if he presumed to disturb the company by his presence, he would be seized where he stood, and, without further inquiry, committed to the provost-marshal for instant execution;—on which account, all persons were warned carefully to forbear from intrusions of simple curiosity, since in the hurry of the moment it might be difficult to make the requisite distinctions."

It was anticipated that this insulting notice would not long go without an answer from The Masque. Accordingly, on the following morning, a placard, equally conspicuous, was posted up in the same public places, side by side with that to which it replied. It was couched in the following terms: "That he who ruled by night in Klosterheim could not suppose himself to be excluded from a nocturnal *fête* given by any person in that city. That he must be allowed to believe himself invited by the prince, and would certainly have the honor to accept his highness' obliging summons. With regard to the low personalities addressed to himself, that he could not descend to notice anything of that nature, coming from a man so abject as Adorni, until he should first have cleared himself from the imputation of having been a tailor in Venice at the time of the Spanish conspiracy in 1618, and banished from that city, not for any suspicions that could have settled upon him and his eight journeymen as making up one conspirator, but on account of some professional tricks in making a doublet for the Doge. For the rest, he repeated that he would not fail to meet the Landgrave and his honorable company."

All Klosterheim laughed at this public mortification offered to Adorni's pride; for that minister had incurred the public dislike as a foreigner, and their hatred on the score of private character. Adorni himself foamed at the mouth with rage, impotent for the present, but which he prepared to give deadly effect to at the proper time. But, whilst it laughed, Klosterheim also trembled. Some persons, indeed, were of opinion that the answer of The Masque was a mere sportive effusion of malice or pleasantry from the students, who had suffered so much by his annoyances. But the majority, amongst whom was Adorni himself, thought otherwise. Apart even from the reply, or the insult which had provoked it, the general impression was, that The Masque would not have failed in attending a festival, which, by the very costume which it imposed, offered so favorable a cloak to his own mysterious purposes. In this persuasion, Adorni took all the precautions which personal vengeance and Venetian subtlety could suggest, for availing himself of the single opportunity that would, perhaps, ever be allowed him for entrapping this public enemy, who had now become a private one to himself.

These various incidents had furnished abundant matter for conversation in Klosterheim, and had carried the public expectation to the highest pitch of anxiety, some time before the great evening arrived. Leisure had been allowed for fear, and every possible anticipation of the wildest character to unfold themselves. Hope, even, amongst many was a predominant sensation. Ladies were preparing for hysterics. Cavaliers, besides the swords which they wore as regular articles of dress, were providing themselves with stilettoes against any sudden rencontre hand to hand, or any unexpected surprise. Armorers and furbishers of weapons were as much in request as the more appropriate artists who minister to such festal occasions. These again were summoned to give their professional aid and attendance to an extent so much out of proportion to their numbers and their natural power of exertion, that they were harassed beyond all physical capacity of endurance, and found their ingenuity more heavily taxed to find personal substitutes amongst the trades most closely connected with their own, than in any of the contrivances which more properly fell within the business of their own art. Tailors, horse-milliners, shoemakers, friseurs, drapers, mercers, tradesmen of every description, and servants of every class and denomination, were summoned to a sleepless activity—each in his several vocation, or in some which he undertook by proxy. Artificers who had escaped on political motives from Nuremburg and other imperial cities, or from the sack of Magdeburg, now showed their ingenuity, and their readiness to earn the bread of industry; and if Klosterheim resembled a hive in the close-packed condition of its inhabitants, it was now seen that the resemblance held good hardly less in the industry which, upon a sufficient excitement, it was able to develop. But, in the midst of all this stir, din, and unprecedented activity, whatever occupation each man found for his thoughts or for his hands in his separate employments, all hearts were mastered by one domineering interest—the approaching collision of the Landgrave, before his assembled court, with the mysterious agent who had so long troubled his repose.

CHAPTER XIV

THE day at length arrived; the guards were posted in unusual strength; the pages of honor, and servants in their state-dresses, were drawn up in long and gorgeous files along the sides of the vast Gothic halls, which ran in continued succession from the front of the *schloss* to the more modern saloons in the rear; bands of military music, collected from amongst the foreign prisoners of various nations at Vienna, were stationed in their national costume—Italian, Hungarian, Turkish, or Croatian—in the lofty galleries or corridors which ran round the halls; and the deep thunders of the kettle-drums, relieved by cymbals and wind-instruments, began to fill the mazes of the palace as early as seven o'clock in the evening; for at that hour, according to the custom then established in Germany, such entertainments commenced. Repeated volleys from long lines of musketeers, drawn up in the square, and at the other entrances of the palace, with the deep roar of artillery, announced the arrival of the more distinguished visitors; amongst whom it was rumored that several officers in supreme command from the Swedish camp, already collected in the neighborhood, were this night coming *incognito*—availing themselves of their masques to visit the Landgrave, and improve the terms of their alliance, whilst they declined the risk which they might have brought on themselves by too open a visit, in their own avowed characters and persons, to a town so unsettled in its state of feeling, and so friendly to the emperor, as Klosterheim had notoriously become.

From seven to nine o'clock, in one unbroken line of succession, gorgeous parties streamed along through

the halls, a distance of full half a quarter of a mile, until
they were checked by the barriers erected at the entrance to the first of the entertaining rooms, as the station for examining the tickets of admission. This duty
was fulfilled in a way which, though really rigorous in
the extreme, gave no inhospitable annoyance to the
visitors; the barriers themselves concealed their jealous
purpose of hostility, and in a manner disavowed the
secret awe and mysterious terror which brooded over
the evening, by the beauty of their external appearance.
They presented a triple line of gilt lattice-work, rising to
a great altitude and connected with the fretted roof by
pendent draperies of the most magnificent velvet, intermingled with banners and heraldic trophies suspended
from the ceiling, and at intervals slowly agitated in the
currents which now and then swept these aërial heights.
In the centre of the lattice opened a single gate, on each
side of which were stationed a couple of sentinels armed
to the teeth; and this arrangement was repeated three
times, so rigorous was the vigilance employed. At the
second of the gates, where the bearer of a forged ticket
would have found himself in a sort of trap, with abso-
lutely no possibility of escape, every individual of each
successive party presented his card of admission, and,
fortunately for the convenience of the company, in consequence of the particular precaution used, one moment's inspection sufficed. The cards had been issued to
the parties invited not very long before the time of as-
sembling; consequently, as each was sealed with a private seal of the Landgrave's, sculptured elaborately with
his armorial bearings, forgery would have been next to
impossible.

These arrangements, however, were made rather to
relieve the company from the too powerful terrors
which haunted them, and to possess them from the first
with a sense of security, than for the satisfaction of the

Landgrave or his minister. They were sensible that The Masque had it in his power to command an access from the interior—and this it seemed next to impossible altogether to prevent; nor was *that* indeed the wish of Adorni, but rather to facilitate his admission, and afterwards, when satisfied of his actual presence, to bar up all possibility of retreat. Accordingly, the interior arrangements, though perfectly prepared, and ready to close up at the word of command, were for the present but negligently enforced.

Thus stood matters at nine o'clock, by which time upwards of a thousand persons had assembled; and in ten minutes more an officer reported that the whole twelve hundred were present, without one defaulter.

The Landgrave had not yet appeared, his minister having received the company; nor was he expected to appear for an hour—in reality, he was occupied in political discussion with some of the illustrious *incognitos*. But this did not interfere with the progress of the festival; and at this moment nothing could be more impressive than the far-stretching splendors of the spectacle.

In one immense saloon, twelve hundred cavaliers and ladies, attired in the unrivalled pomp of that age, were arranging themselves for one of the magnificent Hungarian dances, which the emperor's court at Vienna had transplanted to the camp of Wallenstein, and thence to all the great houses of Germany. Bevies of noble women, in every variety of fanciful costume, but in each considerable group presenting deep masses of black or purple velvet, on which, with the most striking advantage of radiant relief, lay the costly pearl ornaments, or the sumptuous jewels, so generally significant in those times of high ancestral pretensions, intermingled with the drooping plumes of martial cavaliers, who presented almost universally the soldierly air of frankness which belongs to active service, mixed with the Castilian *grandezza* that still breathed through the camps of Germany, emanating originally from the magnificent courts of Brussels, of Madrid, and of Vienna, and propagated to this age by the links of Tilly, the Bavarian commander, and Wallenstein, the more than princely commander for the emperor. Figures and habiliments so commanding were of themselves enough to fill the eye and occupy the imagination; but, beyond all this, feelings of awe and mystery, under more shapes than one, brooded over the whole scene, and diffused a tone of suspense and intense excitement throughout the vast assembly. It was known that illustrious strangers were present *incognito*. There now began to be some reason for anticipating a great battle in the neighborhood. The men were now present, perhaps, the very hands were now visibly displayed for the coming dance, which in a few days, or even hours (so rapid were the movements at this period), were to wield the truncheon that might lay the Catholic empire prostrate, or might mould the destiny of Europe for centuries. Even this feeling gave way to one still more enveloped in shades—The Masque! Would he keep his promise, and appear? might he not be there already? might he not even now be moving amongst them? may he not, even at this very moment, thought each person, secretly be near me—or even touching myself—or haunting my own steps?

Yet again thought most people (for at that time hardly anybody affected to be incredulous in matters allied to the supernatural), was this mysterious being liable to touch? Was he not of some impassive nature, inaudible, invisible, impalpable? Many of his escapes, if truly reported, seemed to argue as much. If, then, connected with the spiritual world, was it with the good or the evil in that inscrutable region? But, then, the bloodshed, the torn dresses, the marks of deadly struggle, which remained behind in some of those cases where mysterious disappearances had occurred,—these seemed undeniable arguments of murder, foul and treacherous murder. Every attempt, in short, to penetrate the mystery of this being's nature, proved as abortive as the attempts to intercept his person; and all efforts at applying a solution to the difficulties of the case made the mystery even more mysterious.

These thoughts, however, generally as they pervaded the company, would have given way, for a time at least, to the excitement of the scene; for a sudden clapping of hands from some officers of the household, to enforce attention, and as a signal to the orchestra in one of the galleries, at this moment proclaimed that the dances were on the point of commencing in another half-minute, when suddenly a shriek from a female, and then a loud, tumultuous cry from a multitude of voices, announced some fearful catastrophe; and in the next moment a shout of "Murder!" froze the blood of the timid amongst the company.

CHAPTER XV

So vast was the saloon, that it had been impossible, through the maze of figures, the confusion of colors, and the mingling of a thousand voices, that anything should be perceived distinctly at the lower end of all that was now passing at the upper. Still, so awful is the mystery of life, and so hideous and accursed in man's imagination is every secret extinction of that consecrated lamp, that no news thrills so deeply, or travels so rapidly. Hardly could it be seen in what direction, or through whose communication, yet in less than a minute a movement of sympathizing horror, and uplifted hands, announced that the dreadful news had reached them. A murder, it was said, had been committed in the palace. Ladies began to faint; others hastened away in search of friends; others to learn the news more accurately; and some of the gentlemen, who thought themselves sufficiently privileged by rank, hurried off with a stream of agitated inquirers to the interior of the castle, in search of the scene itself. A few only passed the guard in the first moments of confusion, and penetrated, with the agitated Adorni, through the long and winding passages, into the very scene of the murder. A rumor had prevailed for a moment that the Landgrave was himself the victim; and as the road by which the agitated household conducted them took a direction towards his highness' suite of rooms, at first Adorni had feared that result. Recovering his self-possession, however, at length, he learned that it was the poor old seneschal upon whom the blow had fallen. And he pressed on with more coolness to the dreadful spectacle.

The poor old man was stretched at his length on the floor. It did not seem that he had struggled with the murderer. Indeed, from some appearances, it seemed probable that he had been attacked whilst sleeping; and though he had received three wounds, it was pronounced by a surgeon that one of them (and *that*, from circumstances, the first) had been sufficient to extinguish life. He was discovered by his daughter, a woman who held some respectable place amongst the servants of the castle; and every presumption concurred in fixing the time of the dreadful scene to about one hour before.

"Such, gentlemen, are the acts of this atrocious monster, this Masque, who has so long been the scourge of Klosterheim," said Adorni to the strangers who had accompanied him, as they turned away on their return to the company; "but this very night, I trust, will put a bridle in his mouth."

"God grant it may be so!" said some. But others thought the whole case too mysterious for conjectures, and too solemn to be decided by presumptions. And in the midst of agitated discussions on the scene they had just witnessed, as well as the whole history of The Masque, the party returned to the saloon.

Under ordinary circumstances, this dreadful event would have damped the spirits of the company; as it was, it did but deepen the gloomy excitement which already had possession of all present, and raise a more intense expectation of the visit so publicly announced by The Masque. It seemed as though he had perpetrated this recent murder merely by way of reviving the impression of his own dreadful character in Klosterheim, which might have decayed a little of late, in all its original strength and freshness of novelty; or, as though he wished to send immediately before him an act of atrocity that should form an appropriate herald or harbinger of his own entrance upon the scene.

Dreadful, however, as this deed of darkness was, it seemed of too domestic a nature to exercise any continued influence upon so distinguished an assembly, so numerous, so splendid, and brought together at so distinguished a summons. Again, therefore, the masques prepared to mingle in the dance; again the signal was given; again the obedient orchestra preluded to the coming strains. In a moment more, the full tide of harmony swept along. The vast saloon, and its echoing roof, rang with the storm of music. The masques, with their floating plumes and jewelled caps, glided through the fine mazes of the Hungarian dances. All was one magnificent and tempestuous confusion, overflowing with the luxury of sound and sight, when suddenly, about midnight, a trumpet sounded, the Landgrave entered, and all was hushed. The glittering crowd arranged themselves in a half-circle at the upper end of the room; his highness went rapidly round, saluting the company, and receiving their homage in return. A signal was again made; the music and the dancing were resumed; and such was the animation and the turbulent delight amongst the gayer part of the company, from the commingling of youthful blood with wine, lights, music, and festal conversation, that, with many, all thoughts of the dreadful Masque, who "reigned by night in Klosterheim," had faded before the exhilaration of the moment. Midnight had come; the dreadful apparition had not yet entered; young ladies began timidly to jest upon the subject, though as yet but faintly, and in a tone somewhat serious for a jest; and young cavaliers, who, to do them justice, had derived most part of their terrors from the superstitious view of the case, protested to their partners that if The Masque, on making his appearance, should conduct himself in a manner unbecoming a cavalier, or offensive to the ladies present, they should feel it their duty to chastise him; "though," said they, "with respect to old Adorni, should The Masque think proper to teach him better manners, or even to cane him, we shall not find it necessary to interfere."

Several of the *very* young ladies protested that, of all things, they should like to see a battle between old Adorni and The Masque, "such a love of a quiz that old Adorni is!" whilst others debated whether The Masque would turn out a young man or an old one; and a few elderly maidens mooted the point whether he were likely to be a "single" gentleman, or burdened with a "wife and family." These and similar discussions were increasing in vivacity, and kindling more and more gayety of repartee, when suddenly, with the effect of a funeral knell upon their mirth, a whisper began to circulate that *there was one Masque too many in company.* Persons had been stationed by Adorni in different galleries, with instructions to note accurately the dress of every person in the company; to watch the motions of every one who gave the slightest cause for suspicion, by standing aloof from the rest of the assembly, or by any other peculiarity of manner; but, above all, to count the numbers of the total assembly. This last injunction was more easily obeyed than at first sight seemed possible. At this time the Hungarian dances, which required a certain number of partners to execute the movements of the figure, were of themselves a sufficient register of the precise amount of persons engaged in them. And, as these dances continued for a long time undisturbed, this calculation once made, left no further computation necessary, than simply to take the account of all who stood otherwise engaged. This list, being much the smaller one, was soon made; and the reports of several different observers, stationed in different galleries, and checked by each other, all tallied in reporting a total of just *twelve hundred and one persons*, after every allowance was made for the known members of the Landgrave's suite, who were all unmasqued.

This report was announced with considerable trepidation, in a very audible whisper, to Adorni and the Landgrave. The buzz of agitation attracted instant attention; the whisper was loud enough to catch the ears of several; the news went rapidly kindling through the room that the company was too many by one: all the ladies trembled, their knees shook, their voices failed, they stopped in the very middle of questions, answers halted for their conclusion, and were never more remembered by either party; the very music began to falter, the lights seemed to wane and sicken; for the fact was now too evident that The Masque had kept his appointment, and was at this moment in the room "to meet the Landgrave and his honorable company."

Adorni and the Landgrave now walked apart from

the rest of the household, and were obviously consulting together on the next step to be taken, or on the proper moment for executing one which had already been decided on. Some crisis seemed approaching, and the knees of many ladies knocked together, as they anticipated some cruel or bloody act of vengeance. "O poor Masque!" sighed a young lady, in her tender-hearted concern for one who seemed now at the mercy of his enemies; "Do you think, sir," addressing her partner, "they will cut him to pieces?"—"O, that wicked old Adorni!" exclaimed another; "I know he will stick the poor Masque on one side, and somebody else will stick him on the other; I know he will, because The Masque called him a tailor; do you think he *was* a tailor, sir?"— "Why, really, madam, he walks like a tailor; but, then, he must be a very bad one, considering how ill his own clothes are made; and *that*, you know, is next door to being none at all. But, see, his highness is going to stop the music."

In fact, at that moment the Landgrave made a signal to the orchestra: the music ceased abruptly; and his highness, advancing to the company, who stood eagerly awaiting his words, said: "Illustrious and noble friends! for a very urgent and special cause I will request of you all to take your seats."

The company obeyed, every one sought the chair next to him, or, if a lady, accepted that which was offered by the cavalier at her side. The standers continually diminished. Two hundred were left, one hundred and fifty, eighty, sixty, twenty, till at last they were reduced to two,—both gentlemen, who had been attending upon ladies. They were suddenly aware of their own situation. One chair only remained out of twelve hundred. Eager to exonerate himself from suspicion, each sprang furiously to this seat; each attained it at the same moment, and each possessed himself of part at the same instant. As they happened to be two elderly, corpulent men, the younger cavaliers, under all the restraints of the moment, the panic of the company, and the Landgrave's presence, could not forbear laughing; and the more spirited amongst the young ladies caught the infection.

His highness was little in a temper to brook this levity, and hastened to relieve the joint occupants of the chair from the ridicule of their situation. "Enough!" he exclaimed, "enough! All my friends are requested to resume the situation most agreeable to them; my purpose is answered." The prince was himself standing with all his household, and, as a point of respect, all the company rose. ("*As you were,*" whispered the young soldiers to their fair companions.)

Adorni now came forward. "It is known," said he, "by trials more than sufficient, that some intruder, with the worst intentions, has crept into this honorable company. The ladies present will therefore have the goodness to retire apart to the lower end of the saloon, whilst the noble cavaliers will present themselves in succession to six officers of his highness' household, to whom they will privately communicate their names and quality."

This arrangement was complied with,—not, however, without the exchange of a few flying jests on the part of the younger cavaliers and their fair partners, as they separated for the purpose. The cavaliers, who were rather more than five hundred in number, went up as they were summoned by the number marked upon their cards of admission, and, privately communicating with some one of the officers appointed, were soon told off, and filed away to the right of the Landgrave, waiting for the signal which should give them permission to rejoin their parties.

All had been now told off, within a score. These were clustered together in a group; and in that group undoubtedly was The Masque. Every eye was converged upon this small knot of cavaliers; each of the spectators, according to his fancy, selected the one who came nearest in dress, or in personal appearance, to his preconceptions of that mysterious agent. Not a word was uttered, not a whisper; hardly a robe was heard to rustle, or a feather to wave.

The twenty were rapidly reduced to twelve, these to six, the six to four—three—two; the tale of the invited was complete, and one man remained behind. That was, past doubting, The Masque!

CHAPTER XVI

"There stands he that governs Klosterheim by night!" thought every cavalier, as he endeavored to pierce the gloomy being's concealment with penetrating eyes, or, by scrutiny ten times repeated, to unmasque the dismal secrets which lurked beneath his disguise. "There stands the gloomy murderer!" thought another. "There stands the poor detected criminal," thought the pitying young ladies, "who in the next moment must lay bare his breast to the Landgrave's musketeers."

The figure, meantime, stood tranquil and collected, apparently not in the least disturbed by the consciousness of his situation, or the breathless suspense of more than a thousand spectators of rank and eminent station, all bending their looks upon himself. He had been leaning against a marble column, as if wrapped up in reverie, and careless of everything about him. But when the dead silence announced that the ceremony was closed, that he only remained to answer for himself, and upon palpable proof—evidence not to be gainsayed—incapable of answering satisfactorily; when, in

fact, it was beyond dispute that here was at length revealed, in bodily presence, before the eyes of those
whom he had so long haunted with terrors, The Masque
of Klosterheim,—it was naturally expected that now, at
least, he would show alarm and trepidation; that he
would prepare for defence, or address himself to instant flight.

Far otherwise! Cooler than any one person beside in
the saloon, he stood, like the marble column against
which he had been reclining, upright, massy, and imperturbable. He was enveloped in a voluminous mantle,
which, at this moment, with a leisurely motion, he suffered to fall at his feet, and displayed a figure in which
the grace of an Antinous met with the columnar
strength of a Grecian Hercules,—presenting, in its *tout
ensemble,* the majestic proportions of a Jupiter. He
stood—a breathing statue of gladiatorial beauty,
towering above all who were near him, and eclipsing the
noblest specimens of the human form which the martial
assembly presented. A buzz of admiration arose, which
in the following moment was suspended by the dubious
recollections investing his past appearances, and the terror which waited even on his present movements. He
was armed to the teeth; and he was obviously preparing
to move.

Not a word had yet been spoken; so tumultuous was
the succession of surprises, so mixed and conflicting the
feelings, so intense the anxiety. The arrangement of the
groups was this: At the lower half of the room, but
starting forward in attitudes of admiration or suspense,
were the ladies of Klosterheim. At the upper end, in the
centre, one hand raised to bespeak attention, was The
Masque of Klosterheim. To his left, and a little behind
him, with a subtle Venetian countenance, one hand
waving back a half file of musketeers, and the other
raised as if to arrest the arm of The Masque, was the

wily minister Adorni, creeping nearer and nearer with a stealthy stride. To his right was the great body of Klosterheim cavaliers, a score of students and young officers pressing forward to the front; but in advance of the whole, the Landgrave of X—, haughty, lowering, and throwing out looks of defiance. These were the positions and attitudes in which the first discovery of The Masque had surprised them; and these they still retained. Less dignified spectators were looking downwards from the galleries.

"Surrender!" was the first word by which silence was broken; it came from the Landgrave.

"Or die!" exclaimed Adorni.

"He dies in any case," rejoined the prince.

The Masque still raised his hand with the action of one who bespeaks attention. Adorni he deigned not to notice. Slightly inclining his head to the Landgrave, in a tone to which it might be the headdress of elaborate steel work that gave a sepulchral tone, he replied:

"The Masque, who rules Klosterheim by night, surrenders not. He can die. But first he will complete the ceremony of the night; he will reveal himself."

"That is superfluous," exclaimed Adorni; "we need no further revelations. Seize him, and lead him out to death!"

"Dog of an Italian!" replied The Masque, drawing a dag from his belt, "die first yourself!" And so saying, he slowly turned and levelled the barrel at Adorni, who fled with two bounds to the soldiers in the rear. Then, withdrawing the weapon hastily, he added, in a tone of cool contempt, "Or bridle that coward's tongue."

But this was not the minister's intention. "Seize him!" he cried again impetuously to the soldiers, laying his hand on the arm of the foremost, and pointing them forward to their prey.

"No!" said the Landgrave, with a commanding voice;

"halt! I bid you." Something there was in the tone, or it might be that there was something in his private recollections, or something in the general mystery, which promised a discovery that he feared to lose by the too precipitate vengeance of the Italian. "What is it, mysterious being, that you would reveal? Or who is it that you now believe interested in your revelations?"

"Yourself.—Prince, it would seem that you have me at your mercy: wherefore, then, the coward haste of this Venetian hound? I am one; you are many. Lead me then, out; shoot me. But no: freely I entered this hall; freely I will leave it. If I must die, I will die as a soldier. Such I am; and neither runagate from a foreign land, nor"—turning to Adorni—"a base mechanic."

"But a murderer!" shrieked Adorni: "but a murderer; and with hands yet reeking from innocent blood!"

"Blood, Adorni, that I will yet avenge.—Prince, you demand the nature of my revelations. I will reveal my name, my quality, and my mission."

"And to whom?"

"To yourself, and none beside. And, as a pledge for the sincerity of my discoveries, I will first of all communicate a dreadful secret, known, as you fondly believe, to none but your highness. Prince, dare you receive my revelations?"

Speaking thus, the Masque took one step to the rear, turning his back upon the room, and by a gesture signified his wish that the Landgrave should accompany him. But at this motion ten or a dozen of the foremost among the young cavaliers started forward in advance of the Landgrave, in part forming a half-circle about his person, and in part commanding the open doorway.

"He is armed!" they exclaimed; "and trebly armed: will your highness approach him too nearly?"

"I fear him not," said the Landgrave, with something of a contemptuous tone.

"Wherefore should you fear me?" retorted The Masque, with a manner so tranquil and serene as involuntarily to disarm suspicion. "Were it possible that I should seek the life of any man here in particular, in that case (pointing to the fire-arms in his belt), why should I need to come nearer? Were it possible that any should find in my conduct here a motive to a personal vengeance upon myself, which of you is not near enough? Has your highness the courage to trample on such terrors?"

Thus challenged, as it were, to a trial of his courage before the assembled rank of Klosterheim, the Landgrave waved off all who would have stepped forward officiously to his support. If he felt any tremors, he was now sensible that pride and princely honor called upon him to dissemble them. And probably, that sort of tremors which he felt in reality did not point in a direction to which physical support, such as was now tendered, could have been available. He hesitated no longer, but strode forward to meet The Masque. His highness and The Masque met near the archway of the door, in the very centre of the groups.

With a thrilling tone, deep, piercing, full of alarm, The Masque began thus:

"To win your confidence, forever to establish credit with your highness, I will first of all reveal the name of that murderer who this night dared to pollute your palace with an old man's blood. Prince, bend your ear a little this way."

With a shudder, and a visible effort of self-command, the Landgrave inclined his ear to The Masque who added,—

"Your highness will be shocked to hear it:" then, in a lower tone, "Who could have believed it?—It was—." All was pronounced clearly and strongly, except the last word—the name of the murderer; *that* was made audible only to the Landgrave's ear.

Sudden and tremendous was the effect upon the prince: he reeled a few paces off; put his hand to the hilt of his sword; smote his forehead; threw frenzied looks upon The Masque,—now half imploring, now dark with vindictive wrath. Then succeeded a pause of profoundest silence, during which all the twelve hundred visitors, whom he had himself assembled as if expressly to make them witnesses of this extraordinary scene, and of the power with which a stranger could shake him to and fro in a tempestuous strife of passions, were looking and hearkening with senses on the stretch to pierce the veil of silence and of distance. At last the Landgrave mastered his emotion sufficiently to say, "Well, sir, what next?"

"Next comes a revelation of another kind; and I warn you, sir, that it will not be less trying to the nerves. For this first I needed your ear; now I shall need your eyes. Think again, prince, whether you will stand the trial."

"Pshaw! sir, you trifle with me; again I tell you——" But here the Landgrave spoke with an affectation of composure, and with an effort that did not escape notice;—"again I tell you that I fear you not. Go on."

"Then come forward a little, please your highness, to the light of this lamp." So saying, with a step or two in advance, he drew the prince under the powerful glare of a lamp suspended near the great archway of entrance from the interior of the palace. Both were now standing with their faces entirely averted from the spectators. Still more effectually, however, to screen himself from any of those groups on the left, whose advanced position gave them somewhat more the advantage of an oblique aspect, The Masque, at this moment, suddenly drew up, with his left hand, a short Spanish mantle which depended from his shoulders, and now gave him the benefit of a lateral screen. Then, so far as the company behind them could guess at his act, unlocking with his right hand and raising the masque which shrouded his mysterious features, he shouted aloud, in a voice that rang clear through every corner of the vast saloon, "Landgrave, for crimes yet unrevealed, I summon you, in twenty days, before a tribunal where there is no shield but innocence!" and at that moment turned his countenance full upon the prince.

With a yell, rather than a human expression of terror, the Landgrave fell, as if shot by a thunderbolt, stretched at his full length upon the ground, lifeless apparently, and bereft of consciousness or sensation. A sympathetic cry of horror arose from the spectators. All rushed towards The Masque. The young cavaliers, who had first stepped forward as volunteers in the Landgrave's defence, were foremost, and interposed between The Masque and the outstretched arms of Adorni, as if eager to seize him first. In an instant a sudden and dense cloud of smoke arose, nobody knew whence. Repeated discharges of fire-arms were heard resounding from the doorway and the passages; these increased the smoke and the confusion. Trumpets sounded through the corridors. The whole archway, under which The Masque and the Landgrave had been standing, became choked up with soldiery, summoned by the furious alarms that echoed through the palace. All was one uproar and chaos of masques, plumes, helmets, halberds, trumpets, gleaming sabres, and the fierce faces of soldiery forcing themselves through the floating drapery of smoke that now filled the whole upper end of the saloon. Adorni was seen in the midst, raving fruitlessly. Nobody heard, nobody listened. Universal panic had seized the household, the soldiery, and the company. Nobody understood exactly for what purpose the tumult had commenced—in what direction it tended. Some tragic catastrophe was reported from mouth to mouth: nobody knew what. Some said the Landgrave had been assassinated; some, The Masque; some asserted that both had perished under reciprocal assaults. More believed that The Masque had proved to be of that supernatural order of beings, with which the prevailing opinions of Klosterheim had long classed him; and that, upon raising his disguise, he had revealed to the Landgrave the fleshless skull of some forgotten tenant of the grave. This indeed seemed to many the only solution that, whilst it fell in with the prejudices and superstitions of the age, was of a nature to account for that tremendous effect which the discovery had produced upon the Landgrave. But it was one that naturally could be little calculated to calm the agitations of the public prevailing at this moment. This spread contagiously. The succession of alarming events,—the murder, the appearance of The Masque, his subsequent extraordinary behavior, the overwhelming impression upon the Landgrave, which had formed the catastrophe of this scenical exhibition,—the consternation of the great Swedish officers, who were spending the night in Klosterheim, and reasonably suspected that the tumult might be owing to the sudden detection of their own *incognito*, and that, in consequence, the populace of this imperial city were suddenly rising to arms; the endless distraction and counter-action of so many thousand persons—visitors, servants, soldiery, household—all hurrying to the same point, and bringing assistance to a danger of which nobody knew the origin, nobody the nature, nobody the issue; multitudes commanding where all obedience was forgotten, all subordination had gone to wreck;—these circumstances of distraction united to sustain a scene of absolute frenzy in the castle, which, for more than half an hour, the dense columns of smoke aggravated alarmingly, by raising, in many quarters, additional terrors of fire. And when, at last, after infinite exertions, the soldiery had deployed into the ball-room and the adjacent apartments of state, and had succeeded, at the point of the pike, in establishing a safe egress for the twelve hundred visitors, it was then first ascertained that all traces of The Masque had been lost in the smoke and subsequent confusion; and that, with his usual good fortune, he had succeeded in baffling his pursuers.

CHAPTER XVII

MEANTIME the Lady Paulina had spent her time in secret grief, inconsolable for the supposed tragical fate of Maximilian. It was believed that he had perished. This opinion had prevailed equally amongst his friends, and the few enemies whom circumstances had made him. Supposing even that he had escaped with life from the action, it seemed inevitable that he should have fallen into the hands of the bloody Holkerstein; and under circumstances which would point him out to the vengeance of that cruel ruffian as having been the leader in the powerful resistance which had robbed him of his prey.

Stung with the sense of her irreparable loss, and the premature grief which had blighted her early hopes, Paulina sought her refuge in solitude, and her consolations in religion. In the convent where she had found a home, the ceremonies of the Roman Catholic service were maintained with the strictness and the pomp suitable to its ample endowments. The emperor had himself, as well as several of his progenitors, been a liberal benefactor to this establishment. And a lady of his house, therefore, recommended by a special introduction from the emperor to the attentions of the lady abbess, was sure of meeting kindness and courtesy in every possible shape which could avail to mitigate her sorrow. The abbess, though a bigot, was a human being, with strong human sensibilities; and in both characters she was greatly pleased with the Lady Paulina. On the one hand, her pride, as the head of a religious establishment, was flattered by the extreme regularity of the Lady Paulina in conforming to the ritual of her house; this example of spiritual obedience and duty seemed peculiarly edifying in a person of such distinguished rank. On the other hand, her womanly sensibilities were touched by the spectacle of early and unmerited sorrow in one so eminent for her personal merits, for her extreme beauty, and the winning sweetness of her manners. Hence she readily offered to the young countess all the attentions and marks of sympathy which her retiring habits permitted, and every species of indulgence compatible with the spirit of the institution.

The whole convent, nuns as well as strangers, taking their tone from the abbess, vied with each other in attentions to Paulina. But, whilst acknowledging their kindness, she continued to shrink from all general intercourse with the society about her. Her attendance was constant at the matins and at vespers; not unfrequently even at the midnight service; but dejection was too rooted in her heart, to allow her any disposition to enter into the amusements or mixed society which the convent at that time offered.

Many noble strangers had been allowed to take up their quarters in the convent. With some of these the abbess was connected by blood; with others, by ties of ancient friendship. Most of this party composed a little society apart from the rest and continued to pursue those amusements or occupations which properly belonged to their stations and quality, but by their too worldly nature were calculated to exclude the religious members of the institution from partaking in them. To this society Paulina received frequent invitations; which, however, she declined so uniformly, that at length all efforts ceased to draw her from the retirement which she so manifestly adhered to from choice. The motives of her dejection became known throughout the convent, and were respected; and it was now reported amongst them, from her aversion to society as well as her increasing devotion, that the Lady Paulina would soon take the veil.

Amongst the strangers was one, a lady of mature age, with beauty still powerful enough to fascinate all beholders, who seemed to survey Paulina with an interest far beyond that of curiosity or simple admiration. Sorrow might be supposed the common bond which connected them; for there were rumors amongst the sisterhood of St. Agnes that this lady had suffered afflictions heavier than fell to an ordinary lot in the course of the war which now desolated Germany. Her husband (it was said), of whom no more was known than that he was some officer of high rank, had perished by the hand of violence; a young daughter, the only child of two or three who remained to her, had been carried off in infancy, and no traces remained of her subsequent fate. To these misfortunes was added the loss of her estates and rank, which, in some mysterious way, were supposed to be withheld from her by one of those great oppressors whom war and the policy of great allies had aggrandized. It was supposed even that for the means of subsistence of herself, and a few faithful attendants, she was indebted to the kindness of the lady abbess, with whom she was closely connected by ancient friendship.

In this tale there were many inaccuracies mixed up with the truth. It was true that, in some one of the many dire convulsions which had passed from land to land since the first outbreak of the Bohemian troubles, in

1618, and which had covered with a veil of political pretexts so many local acts of private family feud and murderous treason, this lady had been deprived of her husband by a violent death under circumstances which still seemed mysterious. But the fate of her children, if any had survived the calamity which took off her husband, was unknown to everybody except her confidential protectress, the lady abbess. By permission of this powerful friend, who had known her from infancy, and through the whole course of her misfortunes, she was permitted to take up her abode in the convent, under special privileges, and was there known by the name of Sister Madeline.

The intercourse of the Sister Madeline with the lady abbess was free and unreserved. At all hours they entered each other's rooms with the familiarity of sisters; and it might have been thought that in every respect they stood upon the equal footing of near relatives, except that occasionally in the manner of the abbess was traced, or imagined, a secret air of deference towards the desolate Sister Madeline, which, as it was not countenanced at all by their present relations to each other, left people at liberty to build upon it a large superstructure of romantic conjectures.

Sister Madeline was as regular in her attendance upon prayers as Paulina. There, if nowhere else, they were sure of meeting; and in no long time it became evident that the younger lady was an object of particular interest to the elder. When the sublime fugues of the old composers for the organ swelled upon the air, and filled the vast aisles of the chapel with their floating labyrinths of sound, attention to the offices of the church service being suspended for the time, the Sister Madeline spent the interval in watching the countenance of Paulina. Invariably at this period her eyes settled upon the young countess, and appeared to court

some return of attention, by the tender sympathy which
her own features expressed with the grief too legibly
inscribed upon Paulina's. For some time Paulina, absorbed by her own thoughts, failed to notice this very
particular expression of attention and interest. Accustomed to the gaze of crowds, as well on account of her
beauty as her connection with the imperial house, she
found nothing new or distressing in this attention to
herself. After some time, however, observing herself
still haunted by the sister's furtive glances, she found
her own curiosity somewhat awakened in return. The
manners of Sister Madeline were too dignified, and her
face expressed too much of profound feeling, and
traces too inextinguishable of the trials through which
she had passed, to allow room for any belief that she was
under the influence of an ordinary curiosity. Paulina
was struck with a confused feeling, that she looked upon
features which had already been familiar to her heart,
though disguised in Sister Madeline by age, by sex, and
by the ravages of grief. She had the appearance of having passed her fiftieth year; but it was probable that,
spite of a brilliant complexion, secret sorrow had
worked a natural effect in giving to her the appearance
of age more advanced by seven or eight years than she
had really attained. Time, at all events, if it had carried
off forever her youthful graces, neither had nor seemed
likely to destroy the impression of majestic beauty
under eclipse and wane. No one could fail to read the
signs by which the finger of nature announces a great
destiny, and a mind born to command.

Insensibly the two ladies had established a sort of intercourse by looks; and at length, upon finding that the
Sister Madeline mixed no more than herself in the general society of Klosterheim, Paulina had resolved to seek
the acquaintance of a lady whose deportment announced that she would prove an interesting acquaint-

ance, whilst her melancholy story and the expression of her looks were a sort of pledges that she would be found a sympathizing friend.

She had already taken some steps towards the attainment of her wishes, when, unexpectedly, on coming out from the vesper service, the Sister Madeline placed herself by the side of Paulina, and they walked down one of the long side-aisles together. The saintly memorials about them, the records of everlasting peace which lay sculptured at their feet, and the strains which still ascended to heaven from the organ and the white-robed choir,—all speaking of a rest from trouble so little to be found on earth, and so powerfully contrasting with the desolations of poor, harassed Germany,—affected them deeply, and both burst into tears. At length the elder lady spoke.

"Daughter, you keep your faith piously with him whom you suppose dead."

Paulina started. The other continued—

"Honor to young hearts that are knit together by ties so firm that even death has no power to dissolve them! Honor to the love which can breed so deep a sorrow! Yet, even in this world, the good are not *always* the unhappy. I doubt not that, even now at vespers, you forgot not to pray for him that would willingly have died for you."

"O, gracious lady! when—when have I forgot that? What other prayer, what other image, is ever at my heart?"

"Daughter, I could not doubt it; and Heaven sometimes sends answers to prayers when they are least expected; and to yours it sends this through me."

With these words she stretched out a letter to Paulina, who fainted with sudden surprise and delight, on recognizing the hand of Maximilian.

CHAPTER XVIII

It was, indeed, the handwriting of her lover; and the
first words of the letter, which bore a recent date, announced his safety and his recovered health. A rapid
sketch of all which had befallen him since they had last
parted informed her that he had been severely
wounded in the action with Holkerstein's people, and
probably to that misfortune had been indebted for his
life; since the difficulty of transporting him on horse-
back, when unable to sit upright, had compelled the
party charged with his care to leave him for the night at
Waldenhausen. From that place he had been carried off
in the night-time to a small imperial garrison in the
neighborhood by the care of two faithful servants, who
had found little difficulty in first intoxicating, and then
overpowering, the small guard judged sufficient for a
prisoner so completely disabled by his wounds. In this
garrison he had recovered; had corresponded with
Vienna; had concerted measures with the emperor and
was now on the point of giving full effect to their plans,
at the moment when certain circumstances should arise
to favor the scheme. What these were, he forbore
designedly to say in a letter which ran some risk of
falling into the enemy's hands; but he bade Paulina
speedily to expect a great change for the better, which
would put it in their power to meet without restraint or
fear; and concluded by giving utterance in the fondest
terms to a lover's hopes and tenderest anxieties.

Paulina had scarcely recovered from the tumultuous
sensations of pleasure, and sudden restoration to hope,
when she received a shock in the opposite direction,
from a summons to attend the Landgrave. The lan-

guage of the message was imperative, and more peremptory than had ever before been addressed to herself, a lady of the imperial family. She knew the Landgrave's character and his present position; both these alarmed her, when connected with the style and language of his summons. For *that* announced distinctly enough that his resolution had been now taken to commit himself to a bold course; no longer to hang doubtfully between two policies, but openly to throw himself into the arms of the emperor's enemies. In one view, Paulina found a benefit to her spirits from this haughtiness of the Landgrave's message. She was neither proud, nor apt to take offence. On the contrary, she was gentle and meek; for the impulses of youth and elevated birth had in her been chastened by her early acquaintance with great national calamities, and the enlarged sympathy which that had bred with her fellow-creatures of every rank. But she felt that, in this superfluous expression of authority, the Landgrave was at the same time infringing on the rights of hospitality, and her own privileges of sex. Indignation at his unmanly conduct gave her spirits to face him, though she apprehended a scene of violence, and had the more reason to feel the trepidations of uncertainty because she very imperfectly comprehended his purposes as respected herself.

These were not easily explained. She found the Landgrave pacing the room with violence. His back was turned her as she entered; but, as the usher announced loudly, on her entrance, "The Countess Paulina of Hohenhelder," he turned impetuously, and advanced to meet her. With the Landgrave, however irritated, the first impulse was to comply with the ceremonious observances that belonged to his rank. He made a cold obeisance, whilst an attendant placed a seat; and then motioning to all present to withdraw, began to unfold the causes which had called for Lady Paulina's presence.

So much art was mingled with so much violence, that for some time Paulina gathered nothing of his real purposes. Resolved, however, to do justice to her own insulted dignity, she took the first opening which offered, to remonstrate with the Landgrave on the needless violence of his summons. His serene highness wielded the sword in Klosterheim, and could have no reason for anticipating resistance to his commands.

"The Lady Paulina, then, distinguishes between the power and the right? I expected as much."

"By no means; she knew nothing of the claimants to either. She was a stranger, seeking only hospitality in Klosterheim, which apparently was violated by unprovoked exertions of authority."

"But the laws of hospitality," replied the Landgrave, "press equally on the guest and the host. Each has his separate duties. And the Lady Paulina in the character of guest, violated hers from the moment when she formed cabals in Klosterheim and ministered to the fury of conspirators."

"Your ear, sir, is abused; I have not so much as stepped beyond the precincts of the convent in which I reside, until this day in paying obedience to your highness' mandate."

"That may be; and that may argue only the more caution and subtlety. The personal presence of a lady, so distinguished in her appearance as the Lady Paulina, at any resort of conspirators or intriguers, would have published too much the suspicions to which such a countenance would be liable. But in writing have you dispersed nothing calculated to alienate the attachment of my subjects?"

The Lady Paulina shook her head; she knew not even in what direction the Landgrave's suspicions pointed.

"As, for example, this—does the Lady Paulina recognize this particular paper?"

Saying this, he drew forth from a portfolio a letter or paper of instructions, consisting of several sheets, to which a large official seal was attached. The countess glanced her eye over it attentively; in one or two places the words *Maximilian* and *Klosterheim* attracted her attention; but she felt satisfied at once that she now saw it for the first time.

"Of this paper," she said, at length, in a determined tone, "I know nothing. The handwriting I believe I may have seen before. It resembles that of one of the emperor's secretaries. Beyond that, I have no means of even conjecturing its origin."

"Beware, madam, beware how far you commit yourself. Suppose now this paper were actually brought in one of your ladyship's mails, amongst your own private property."

"That may very well be," said Lady Paulina, "and yet imply no falsehood on my part. Falsehood! I disdain such an insinuation; your highness has been the first person who ever dared to make it." At that moment she called to mind the robbery of her carriage at Waldenhausen. Coloring deeply with indignation, she added, "Even in the case, sir, which you have supposed, as unconscious bearer of this or any other paper, I am still innocent of the intentions which such an act might argue in some people. I am as incapable of offending in that way as I shall always be of disavowing any of my own acts, according to your ungenerous insinuation. But now, sir, tell me how far those may be innocent who have possessed themselves of a paper carried, as your highness alleges, among my private baggage. Was it for a prince to countenance a robbery of that nature, or to appropriate its spoils?"

The blood rushed to the Landgrave's temples. "In these times, young lady, petty rights of individuals give way to state necessities. Neither are there any such rights of individuals in bar of such an inquisition. They are forfeited, as I told you before, when the guest forgets his duties. But (and here he frowned), it seems to me, countess, that you are now forgetting your situation; not I, remember, but yourself, are now placed on trial."

"Indeed!" said the countess, "of that I was certainly not aware. Who, then, is my accuser, who my judge? Or is it in your serene highness that I see both?"

"Your accuser, Lady Paulina, is the paper I have shown you, a treasonable paper. Perhaps I have others to bring forward of the same bearing. Perhaps this is sufficient."

The Lady Paulina grew suddenly sad and thoughtful. Here was a tyrant, with matter against her, which, even to an unprejudiced judge, might really wear some face of plausibility. The paper had perhaps really been one of those plundered from her carriage. It might really contain matter fitted to excite disaffection against the Landgrave's government. Her own innocence of all participation in the designs which it purposed to abet might find no credit; or might avail her not at all in a situation so far removed from the imperial protection. She had in fact unadvisedly entered a city, which, at the time of her entrance, might be looked upon as neutral, but since then had been forced into the ranks of the emperor's enemies, too abruptly to allow of warning or retreat. This was her exact situation. She saw her danger; and again apprehended that, at the very moment of recovering her lover from the midst of perils besetting *his* situation, she might lose him by the perils of her own.

The Landgrave watched the changes of her countenance, and read her thoughts.

"Yes," he said, at length, "your situation is one of peril. But take courage. Confess freely, and you have everything to hope for from my clemency."

"Such clemency," said a deep voice from some remote quarter of the room, "as the wolf shows to the lamb."

Paulina started, and the Landgrave looked angry and perplexed. "Within, there!" he cried loudly to the attendants in the next room. "I will no more endure these insults," he exclaimed. "Go instantly, take a file of soldiers; place them at all the outlets, and search the rooms adjoining—above, and below. Such mummery is insufferable."

The voice replied again, "Landgrave, you search in vain. Look to yourself! young Max is upon you!"

"This babbler," said the Landgrave, making an effort to recover his coolness, "reminds me well; that adventurer, young Maximilian—who is he? whence comes he? by whom authorized?"

Paulina blushed; but, roused by the Landgrave's contumelious expressions applied to her lover, she replied, "He is no adventurer; nor was ever in that class; the emperor's favor is not bestowed upon such."

"Then, what brings him to Klosterheim? For what is it that he would trouble the repose of this city?"

Before Paulina could speak in rejoinder, the voice, from a little further distance, replied, audibly, "For his rights! See that you, Landgrave, make no resistance."

The prince arose in fury; his eyes flashed fire, he clenched his hands in impotent determination. The same voice had annoyed him on former occasions, but never under circumstances which mortified him so deeply. Ashamed that the youthful countess should be a witness of the insults put upon him, and seeing that it was in vain to pursue his conversation with her further in a situation which exposed him to the sarcasms of a third person, under no restraint of fear or partiality, he adjourned the further prosecution of his inquiry to another opportunity, and for the present gave her leave to depart; a license which she gladly availed herself of, and retired in fear and perplexity.

CHAPTER XIX

I⟨T⟩ was dark as Paulina returned to her convent. Two servants of the Landgrave's preceded her with torches to the great gates of St. Agnes, which was at a very short distance. At that point she entered within the shelter of the convent gates, and the prince's servants left her at her own request. No person was now within call but a little page of her own, and perhaps the porter at the convent. But after the first turn in the garden of St. Agnes, she might almost consider herself as left to her own guardianship; for the little boy, who followed her, was too young to afford her any effectual help. She felt sorry, as she surveyed the long avenue of ancient trees, which was yet to be traversed before she entered upon the cloisters, that she should have dismissed the servants of the Landgrave. These gardens were easily scaled from the outside, and a ready communication existed between the remotest parts of this very avenue and some of the least reputable parts of Klosterheim. The city now overflowed with people of every rank; and amongst them were continually recognized, and occasionally challenged, some of the vilest deserters from the imperial camps. Wallenstein himself, and other imperial commanders, but, above all, Holk, had attracted to their standards the very refuse of the German jails and, allowing an unlimited license of plunder during some periods of their career, had themselves evoked a fiendish spirit of lawless aggression and spoliation, which afterwards they had found it impossible to exorcise within its former limits. People were everywhere obliged to be on their guard, not alone (as heretofore) against the military tyrant or freebooter, but also against the private servants whom they hired into their service. For some time back, suspicious persons had been seen strolling at dusk in the gardens of St. Agnes, or even intruding into the cloisters. Then the recollection of The Masque, now in the very height of his mysterious career, flashed upon Paulina's thoughts. Who knew his motives, or the principle of his mysterious warfare— which, at any rate, in its mode had latterly been marked by bloodshed? As these things came rapidly into her mind, she trembled more from fear than from the wintry wind, which now blew keenly and gustily through the avenue.

The gardens of St. Agnes were extensive, and Paulina yet wanted two hundred yards of reaching the cloisters, when she observed a dusky object stealing along the margin of a little pool, which in parts lay open to the walk, whilst in others, where the walk receded from the water, the banks were studded with thickets of tall shrubs. Paulina stopped and observed the figure, which she was soon satisfied must be that of a man. At times he rose to his full height; at times he cowered downwards amongst the bushes. That he was not merely seeking a retreat became evident from this, that the best road for such a purpose lay open to him in the opposite direction; that he was watching herself, also, became probable from the way in which he seemed to regulate his own motions by hers. At length, whilst Paulina hesitated, in some perplexity whether to go forward or to retreat towards the porter's lodge, he suddenly plunged into the thickest belt of shrubs, and left the road clear. Paulina seized the moment, and, with a palpitating heart, quickened her steps towards the cloister.

She had cleared about one half of the way without obstruction, when suddenly a powerful grasp seized her by the shoulder.

"Stop, lady!" said a deep, coarse voice; "stop! I mean

no harm. Perhaps I bring your ladyship what will be welcome news."

"But why here?" exclaimed Paulina; "wherefore do you alarm me thus? O, heavens! your eyes are wild and fierce; say, is it money that you want?"

"Perhaps I do. To the like of me, lady, you may be sure that money never comes amiss; but that is not my errand. Here is what will make all clear;" and, as he spoke, he thrust his hand into the huge pocket within the horseman's cloak which enveloped him. Instead of the pistol or dag, which Paulina anticipated, he drew forth a large packet, carefully sealed. Paulina felt so much relieved at beholding this pledge of the man's pacific intentions, that she eagerly pressed her purse into his hand, and was hastening to leave him, when the man stopped her to deliver a verbal message from his master, requesting earnestly that, if she concluded to keep the appointment arranged in the letter, she would not be a minute later than the time fixed.

"And who," said Paulina, "is your master?"

"Surely, the general, madam—the young General Maximilian. Many a time and oft have I waited on him when visiting your ladyship at the Wartebrunn. But here I dare not show my face. Der Henker! if the Landgrave knew that Michael Klotz was in Klosterheim, I reckon that all the ladies in St. Agnes could not beg him a reprieve till to-morrow morning."

"Then, villain!" said the foremost of two men, who rushed hastily from the adjoining shrubs, "be assured that the Landgrave does know it. Let this be your warrant!" With these words he fired, and, immediately after, his comrade. Whether the fugitive were wounded could not be known; for he instantly plunged into the water, and, after two or three moments, was heard upon the opposite margin. His pursuers seemed to shrink from this attempt, for they divided and took the oppo-

site extremities of the pool, from the other bank of
which they were soon heard animating and directing
each other through the darkness.

Paulina, confused and agitated, and anxious above all
to examine her letters, took the opportunity of a clear
road, and fled in trepidation to the convent.

CHAPTER XX

THE countess had brought home with her a double
subject of anxiety. She knew not to what result the
Landgrave's purposes were tending; she feared, also,
from this sudden and new method of communication
opened with herself so soon after his previous letter,
that some unexpected bad fortune might now be
threatening her lover. Hastily she tore open the packet,
which manifestly contained something larger than letters. The first article which presented itself was a nun's
veil, exactly on the pattern of those worn by the nuns of
St. Agnes. The accompanying letter sufficiently explained its purpose.

It was in the handwriting, and bore the signature, of
Maximilian. In a few words he told her that a sudden
communication, but from a quarter entirely to be depended on, had reached him of a great danger impending over her from the Landgrave; that, in the present
submission of Klosterheim to that prince's will, instant
flight presented the sole means of delivering her; for
which purpose he would himself meet her in disguise on
the following morning, as early as four o'clock; or, if
that should prove impossible under the circumstances
of the case, would send a faithful servant; that one or
other of them would attend at a particular station, easily
recognized by the description added, in a ruinous part

of the boundary wall, in the rear of the convent garden. A large travelling cloak would be brought, to draw over the rest of her dress; but meanwhile, as a means of passing unobserved through the convent grounds, where the Landgrave's agents were continually watching her motions, the nun's veil was almost indispensable. The other circumstances of the journey would be communicated to her upon meeting. In conclusion, the writer implored Paulina to suffer no scruples of false delicacy to withhold her from a step which had so suddenly become necessary to her preservation; and cautioned her particularly against communicating her intentions to the lady abbess, whose sense of decorum might lead her to urge advice at this moment inconsistent with her safety.

Again and again did Paulina read this agitating letter; again and again did she scrutinize the handwriting, apprehensive that she might be making herself a dupe to some hidden enemy. The handwriting, undoubtedly, had not all the natural freedom which characterized that of Maximilian; it was somewhat stiff in its movement, but not more so than that of his previous letter, in which he had accounted for the slight change from a wound not perfectly healed in his right hand. In other respects the letter seemed liable to no just suspicion. The danger apprehended from the Landgrave tallied with her own knowledge. The convent grounds were certainly haunted, as the letter alleged, by the Landgrave's people; of that she had just received a convincing proof; for, though the two strangers had turned off in pursuit of the messenger who bore Maximilian's letter yet doubtless their original object of attention had been herself; they were then posted to watch her motions, and they had avowed themselves in effect the Landgrave's people. That part of the advice, again, which respected the lady abbess, seemed judicious, on considering the character of that lady, however much at first sight it might warrant some jealousy of the writer's purposes to find him warning her against her best friends. After all, what most disturbed the confidence of Paulina was the countenance of the man who presented the letter. If this man were to be the representative of Maximilian on the following morning, she felt, and was persuaded that she would continue to feel, an invincible repugnance to commit her safety to any such keeping. Upon the whole, she resolved to keep the appointment, but to be guided in her further conduct by circumstances as they should arise at the moment.

That night Paulina's favorite female attendant employed herself in putting into as small a compass as possible the slender wardrobe which they would be able to carry with them. The young countess herself spent the hours in writing to the lady abbess and Sister Madeline, acquainting them with all the circumstances of her interview with the Landgrave, the certain grounds she had for apprehending some great danger in that quarter, and the proposals so unexpectedly made to her on the part of Maximilian for evading it. To ask that they should feel no anxiety on her account, in times which made even a successful escape from danger so very hazardous, she acknowledged would be vain but, in judging of the degree of prudence which she had exhibited on this occasion, she begged them to reflect on the certain dangers which awaited her from the Landgrave; and finally, in excuse for not having sought the advice of so dear a friend as the lady abbess, she enclosed the letter upon which she had acted.

These preparations were completed by midnight, after which Paulina sought an hour or two of repose. At three o'clock were celebrated the early matins, attended by the devouter part of the sisterhood, in the chapel. Paulina and her maid took this opportunity for leaving their chamber, and slipping unobserved amongst the crowd who were hurrying on that summons into the cloisters. The organ was pealing solemnly through the labyrinth of passages which led from the interior of the convent; and Paulina's eyes were suffused with tears, as the gentler recollections of her earlier days, and the peace which belongs to those who have abjured this world and its treacherous promises, arose to her mind, under the influence of the sublime music, in powerful contrast with the tempestuous troubles of Germany— now become so comprehensive, in their desolating sweep, as to involve even herself and others of station as elevated.

CHAPTER XXI

THE convent clock, chiming the quarters, at length announced that they had reached the appointed hour. Trembling with fear and cold, though muffled up in furs, Paulina and her attendant, with their nuns' veils drawn over their head-dress, sallied forth into the garden. All was profoundly dark, and overspread with the stillness of the grave. The lights within the chapel threw a rich glow through the painted windows; and here and there, from a few scattered casements in the vast pile of St. Agnes, streamed a few weak rays from a taper or a lamp, indicating the trouble of a sick bed, or the peace of prayer. But these rare lights did but deepen the massy darkness of all beside; and Paulina, with her attendant, had much difficulty in making her way to the appointed station. Having reached the wall, however, they pursued its windings, certain of meeting no important obstacles, until they attained a part where their progress was impeded by frequent dilapidations. Here they halted, and in low tones communicated their doubts about the precise locality of the station indicated in the letter, when suddenly a man started up from the ground, and greeted them with the words "St. Agnes! all is right," which had been preconcerted as the signal in the letter. This man was courteous and respectful in his manner of speaking, and had nothing of the ruffian voice which belonged to the bearer of the letter. In rapid terms he assured Paulina that "the young general" had not found circumstances favorable for venturing within the walls, but that he would meet her a few miles beyond the city gates; and that at present they had no time to lose. Saying this, he unshaded a dark lantern, which showed them a ladder of ropes, attached to the summit of a wall, which at this point was too low to occasion them much uneasiness or difficulty in ascending. But Paulina insisted previously on hearing something more circumstantial of the manner and style of their escape from the city walls, and in what company their journey would be performed. The man had already done something to conciliate Paulina's confidence by the propriety of his address, which indicated a superior education, and habits of intercourse with people of rank. He explained as much of the plan as seemed necessary for the immediate occasion. A convoy of arms and military stores was leaving the city for the post at Falkenstein. Several carriages, containing privileged persons, to whom the Landgrave or his minister had granted a license, were taking the benefit of an escort over the forest; and a bribe in the proper quarter had easily obtained permission, from the officer on duty at the gates, to suffer an additional carriage to pass as one in a great lady's suite, on the simple condition that it should contain none but females; as persons of that sex were liable to no suspicion of being fugitives from the wrath which was now supposed ready to descend upon the conspirators against the Landgrave.

The explanation reconciled Paulina to the scheme. She felt cheered by the prospect of having other ladies to countenance the mode of her nocturnal journey; and at the worst, hearing this renewed mention of conspirators and punishment, which easily connected itself with all that had passed in her interview with the Landgrave, she felt assured, at any rate, that the dangers she fled from transcended any which she was likely to incur on her route. Her determination was immediately taken. She passed over the wall with her attendant; and they found themselves in a narrow lane, close to the city walls, with none but a few ruinous outhouses on either side. A low whistle from the man was soon answered by the rumbling of wheels; and from some distance, as it seemed, a sort of caleche advanced, drawn by a pair of horses. Paulina and her attendant stepped hastily in, for at the very moment when the carriage drew up a signal-gun was heard; which, as their guide assured them, proclaimed that the escort and the whole train of carriages were at that moment defiling from the city gate. The driver, obeying the directions of the other man, drove off as rapidly as the narrow road and the darkness would allow. A few turns brought them into the great square in front of the *schloss;* from which a few more open streets, traversed at full gallop, soon brought them into the rear of the convoy, which had been unexpectedly embarrassed in its progress to the gate. From the rear, by dexterous management, they gradually insinuated themselves into the centre; and, contrary to their expectations, amongst the press of baggage-wagons, artillery, and travelling equipages, all tumultuously clamoring to push on, as the best chance of evading Holkerstein in the forest, their own unpretending vehicle passed without other notice than a curse from the officer on duty; which, however, they could not presume to appropriate, as it might be supposed equitably distributed amongst all who stopped the road at the moment.

Paulina shuddered as she looked out upon the line of fierce faces, illuminated by the glare of torches, and mingling with horses' heads, and the gleam of sabres; all around her, the roar of artillery wheels; above her head the vast arch of the gates, its broad massy shadows resting below; and in the vista beyond, which the archway defined, a mass of blackness, in which she rather imagined than saw the interminable solitudes of the forest. Soon the gate was closed; their own carriage passed the tardier parts of the convoy; and, with a dozen or two of others, surrounded by a squadron of dragoons, headed the train. Happy beyond measure at the certainty that she had now cleared the gates of Klosterheim, that she was in the wide, open forest, free from a detested tyrant, and on the same side of the gates as her lover, who was doubtless advancing to meet her, she threw herself back in her carriage, and resigned herself to a slumber, which the anxieties and watchings of the night had made more than usually welcome.

The city clocks were now heard in the forest, solemnly knelling out the hour of four. Hardly, however, had Paulina slept an hour, when she was gently awaked by her attendant, who had felt it to be her duty to apprise her lady of the change which had occurred in their situation. They had stopped, it seemed, to attach a pair of leaders to their wheel-horses, and were now advancing at a thundering pace, separated from the rest of the convoy, and surrounded by a small escort of cavalry. The darkness was still intense; and the lights of Klosterheim, which the frequent windings of the road brought often into view, were at this moment conspicuously seen. The castle, from its commanding position, and the Convent of St. Agnes, were both easily traced out by means of the lights gleaming from their long ranges of upper windows. A particular turret, which sprung to an almost aërial altitude above the rest of the building, in which it was generally reported that the Landgrave slept, was more distinguishable than any other part of Klosterheim, from one brilliant lustre which shot its rays through a large oriel window. There at this moment was sleeping that unhappy prince, tyrannical and self-tormenting, whose unmanly fears had menaced her own innocence with so ,much indefinite danger; whom, in escaping, she knew not if she *had* escaped; and whose snares, as a rueful misgiving began to suggest, were perhaps gathering faster about her, with every echo which the startled forest returned to the resounding tread of their flying cavalcade. She leaned back again in the carriage; again she fell asleep; again she dreamed. But her sleep was unrefreshing; her dreams were agitated, confused, and haunted by terrific images. And she awoke repeatedly with her cheerful anticipation continually decaying of speedily (perhaps ever again) rejoining her gallant Maximilian. There was indeed yet a possibility that she might be under the superintending care of her lover. But she secretly felt that she was betrayed. And she wept when she reflected that her own precipitance had facilitated the accomplishment of the plot which had perhaps forever ruined her happiness.

CHAPTER XXII

MEANTIME, Paulina awoke from the troubled slumbers into which her fatigues had thrown her, to find herself still flying along as rapidly as four powerful horses could draw their light burden, and still escorted by a considerable body of the Landgrave's dragoons. She was undoubtedly separated from all the rest of the convoy with whom she had left Klosterheim. It was now apparent, even to her humble attendant, that they were betrayed; and Paulina reproached herself with having voluntarily cooperated with her enemy's stratagems. Certainly the dangers from which she fled were great and imminent; yet still, in Klosterheim, she derived some protection from the favor of the lady abbess. That lady had great powers of a legal nature throughout the city, and still greater influence with a Roman Catholic populace at this particular period, when their prince had laid himself open to suspicions of favoring Protestant allies; and Paulina bitterly bewailed the imprudence which, in removing her from the Convent of St. Agnes, had removed her from her only friends.

It was about noon when the party halted at a solitary house for rest and refreshments. Paulina had heard nothing of the route which they had hitherto taken, nor did she find it easy to collect, from the short and churlish responses of her escort to the few questions she had yet ventured to propose, in what direction their future advance would proceed. A hasty summons bade her alight; and a few steps, under the guidance of a trooper, brought her into a little gloomy wainscoted room, where some refreshments had been already spread upon a table. Adjoining was a small bed-room. And she was desired, with something more like civility than she had yet experienced, to consider both as allotted for the use of herself and servant during the time of their stay, which was expected, however, not to exceed the two or three hours requisite for resting the horses.

But that was an arrangement which depended as much upon others as themselves. And, in fact, a small party, whom the main body of the escort had sent on to patrol the roads in advance, soon returned with the unwelcome news that a formidable corps of imperialists were out reconnoitring in a direction which might probably lead them across their own line of march, in the event of their proceeding instantly. The orders already issued for advance were therefore countermanded; and a resolution was at length adopted by the leader of the party for taking up their abode during the night in their present very tolerable quarters.

Paulina, wearied and dejected, and recoiling naturally from the indefinite prospects of danger before her, was not the least rejoiced at this change in the original plan, by which she benefited at any rate to the extent of a quiet shelter for one night more,—a blessing which the next day's adventures might deny her,—and still more by that postponement of impending evil which is so often welcome to the very firmest minds, when exhausted by toil and affliction. Having this certainty, however, of one night's continuance in her present abode, she requested to have the room made a little more comfortable by the exhilarating blaze of a fire. For this indulgence there were the principal requisites in a hearth and spacious chimney. And an aged crone, probably the sole female servant upon the premises, speedily presented herself with a plentiful supply of wood, and the two supporters, or *andirons* (as they were formerly called), for raising the billets so as to allow the air to circulate from below. There was some difficulty at first in kindling the wood; and the old servant resorted once or twice, after some little apologetic muttering of doubts with herself, to a closet, containing, as Paulina could observe, a considerable body of papers.

The fragments which she left remained strewed upon the ground; and Paulina, taking them up with a careless air, was suddenly transfixed with astonishment on observing that they were undoubtedly in a handwriting familiar to her eye—the handwriting of the most confidential amongst the imperial secretaries. Other recollections now rapidly associated themselves together, which led her hastily to open the closet door;

and there, as she had already half expected, she saw the travelling mail stolen from her own carriage, its lock forced, and the remaining contents (for everything bearing a money value had probably vanished on its first disappearance) lying in confusion. Having made this discovery, she hastily closed the door of the closet, resolved to prosecute her investigations in the night-time; but at present, when she was liable to continual intrusions, to give no occasion for those suspicions, which, once aroused, might end in baffling her design.

Meantime, she occupied herself in conjectures upon the particular course of accident which could have brought the trunk and papers into the situation where she had been fortunate enough to find them. And, with the clue already in her possession, she was not long in making another discovery. She had previously felt some dim sense of recognition, as her eyes wandered over the room, but had explained it away into some resemblance to one or other of the many strange scenes which she had passed through since leaving Vienna. But now, on retracing the furniture and aspect of the two rooms, she was struck with her own inattention, in not having sooner arrived at the discovery that it was their old quarters of Waldenhausen, the very place in which the robbery had been effected, where they had again the prospect of spending the night, and of recovering in part the loss she had sustained.

Midnight came, and the Lady Paulina prepared to avail herself of her opportunities. She drew out the parcel of papers, which was large and miscellaneous in its contents. By far the greater part, as she was happy to observe, were mere copies of originals in the chancery at Vienna; those related to the civic affairs of Klosterheim, and were probably of a nature not to have been acted upon during the predominance of the Swedish interest in the counsels and administration of that city. With the

revival of the imperial cause, no doubt these orders
would be repeated, and with the modifications which
new circumstances and the progress of events would
then have rendered expedient. This portion of the
papers, therefore, Paulina willingly restored to their
situation in the closet. No evil would arise to any party
from their present detention in a place where they were
little likely to attract notice from anybody but the old
lady in her ministries upon the fire. Suspicion would be
also turned aside from herself in appropriating the few
papers which remained. These contained too frequent
mention of a name dear to herself, not to have a considerable value in her eyes; she was resolved, if possible,
to carry them off by concealing them within her bosom;
but, at all events, in preparation for any misfortune that
might ultimately compel her to resign them, she determined, without loss of time, to make herself mistress of
their contents.

One, and the most important of these documents, was
a long and confidential letter from the emperor to the
town council and the chief heads of conventual houses
in Klosterheim. It contained a rapid summary of the
principal events in her lover's life, from his infancy,
when some dreadful domestic tragedy had thrown him
upon the emperor's protection, to his present period of
early manhood, when his own sword and distinguished
talents had raised him to a brilliant name and a high
military rank in the imperial service. What were the
circumstances of that tragedy, as a case sufficiently well
known to those whom he addressed, or to be collected
from accompanying papers, the emperor did not say.
But he lavished every variety of praise upon Maximilian, with a liberality that won tears of delight from the
solitary young lady, as she now sat at midnight looking
over these gracious testimonies to her lover's merit. A
theme so delightful to Paulina could not be unseason-

able at any time; and never did her thoughts revert to
him more fondly than at this moment, when she so
much needed his protecting arm. Yet the emperor, she
was aware, must have some more special motive for en-
larging upon this topic than his general favor to Maximilian. What this could be, in a case so closely connecting the parties to the correspondence on both sides with
Klosterheim, a little interested her curiosity. And, on
looking more narrowly at the accompanying documents, in one which had been most pointedly referred
to by the emperor she found some disclosures on the
subject of her lover's early misfortunes, which, whilst
they filled her with horror and astonishment, elevated
the natural pretensions of Maximilian in point of birth
and descent more nearly to a level with the splendor of
his self-created distinctions; and thus crowned him, who
already lived in her apprehension as the very model of a
hero, with the only advantages that he had ever been
supposed to want—the interest which attaches to unmerited misfortunes, and the splendor of an illustrious
descent.

As she thus sat, absorbed in the story of her lover's
early misfortunes, a murmuring sound of talking attracted her ear, apparently issuing from the closet.
Hastily throwing open the door, she found that a thin
wooden partition, veined with numerous chinks, was
the sole separation between the closet and an adjoining
bed-room. The words were startling, incoherent, and at
times raving. Evidently they proceeded from some patient stretched on a bed of sickness, and dealing with a
sort of horrors in his distempered fancy, worse, it was to
be hoped, than any which the records of his own remembrance could bring before him. Sometimes he
spoke in the character of one who chases a deer in a
forest; sometimes he was close upon the haunches of his
game; sometimes it seemed on the point of escaping

him. Then the nature of the game changed utterly, and became something human; and a companion was suddenly at his side. With him he quarrelled fiercely about their share in the pursuit and capture. "O, my lord, you must not deny it. Look, look! your hands are bloodier than mine. Fie! fie! is there no running water in the forest?—So young as he is, and so noble!—Stand off! he will cover us all with his blood!—O, what a groan was that! It will have broke somebody's heart-strings, I think! It would have broken mine when I was younger. But these wars make us all cruel. Yet you are worse than I am."

Then again, after a pause, the patient seemed to start up in bed, and he cried out, convulsively, "Give me my share, I say. Wherefore must my share be so small? There he comes past again. Now strike—now, now, now! Get his head down, my lord.—He's off, by G—! Now, if he gets out of the forest, two hours will take him to Vienna. And we must go to Rome: where else could we get absolution? O, Heavens! the forest is full of blood; well may our hands be bloody. I see flowers all the way to Vienna: but there is blood below: O what a depth! what a depth!—O! heart, heart!—See how he starts up from his lair!—O! your highness has deceived me! There are a thousand upon one man!"

In such terms he continued to rave, until Paulina's mind was so much harassed with the constant succession of dreadful images and frenzied ejaculations, all making report of a life passed in scenes of horror, bloodshed, and violence, that at length, for her own relief, she was obliged to close the door; through which, however, at intervals, piercing shrieks or half-stifled curses still continued to find their way. It struck her as a remarkable coincidence, that something like a slender thread of connection might be found between the dreadful story narrated in the imperial document, and the delirious ravings of this poor, wretched creature, to whom accident had made her a neighbor for a single night.

Early the next morning Paulina and her servant were summoned to resume their journey; and three hours more of rapid travelling brought them to the frowning fortress of Lovenstein. Their escort, with any one of whom they had found but few opportunities of communicating, had shown themselves throughout gloomy and obstinately silent. They knew not, therefore, to what distance their journey extended. But, from the elaborate ceremonies with which they were here received, and the formal receipt for their persons, which was drawn up and delivered by the governor to the officer commanding their escort, Paulina judged that the castle of Lovenstein would prove to be their final destination.

CHAPTER XXIII

Two days elapsed without any change in Paulina's situation, as she found it arranged upon her first arrival at Lovenstein. Her rooms were not incommodious; but the massy barricades at the doors, the grated windows, and the sentinels who mounted guard upon all the avenues which led to her apartments, satisfied her sufficiently that she was a prisoner.

The third morning after her arrival brought her a still more unwelcome proof of this melancholy truth, in the summons which she received to attend a court of criminal justice on the succeeding day, connected with the tenor of its language. Her heart died within her as she found herself called upon to answer as a delinquent on a charge of treasonable conspiracy with various members of the university of Klosterheim, against the sovereign prince, the Landgrave of X——. Witnesses in exculpation, whom could she produce? Or how defend herself before a tribunal where all alike—judge, evidence, accuser—were in effect one and the same malignant enemy? In what way she could have come to be connected in the Landgrave's mind with a charge of treason against his princely rights, she found it difficult to explain, unless the mere fact of having carried the imperial despatches in the trunks about her carriages were sufficient to implicate her as a secret emissary or agent concerned in the imperial diplomacy. But she strongly suspected that some deep misapprehension existed in the Landgrave's mind; and its origin, she fancied, might be found in the refined knavery of their ruffian host at Waldenhausen, in making his market of the papers which he had purloined. Bringing them forward separately and by piecemeal, he had probably hoped to receive so many separate rewards. But, as it would often happen that one paper was necessary in the way of explanation to another, and the whole, perhaps, were almost essential to the proper understanding of any one, the result would inevitably be grievously to mislead the Landgrave. Further communications, indeed, would have tended to disabuse the prince of any delusions raised in this way. But it was probable, as Paulina had recently learned in passing through Waldenhausen, that the ruffian's illness and delirium had put a stop to any further communication of papers; and thus the misconceptions which he had caused were perpetuated in the Landgrave's mind.

It was on the third day after Paulina's arrival that she was first placed before the court. The presiding officer in this tribunal was the governor of the fortress, a tried soldier, but a ruffian of low habits and cruel nature. He had risen under the Landgrave's patronage, as an adventurer of desperate courage, ready for any service, however disreputable, careless alike of peril or of infamy. In common with many partisan officers, who had sprung from the ranks in this adventurous war, seeing on every side and in the highest quarters, princes as well as supreme commanders, the uttermost contempt of justice and moral principle, he had fought his way to distinction and fortune, through every species of ignoble cruelty. He had passed from service to service, as he saw an opening for his own peculiar interest or merit, everywhere valued as a soldier of desperate enterprise, everywhere abhorred as a man. By birth a Croatian, he had exhibited himself as one of the most savage leaders of that order of barbarians in the sack of Magdeburgh, where he served under Tilly; but, latterly, he had taken service again under his original patron, the Landgrave, who had lured him back to his interest by the rank of general and the governorship of Lovenstein.

This brutal officer, who had latterly lived in a state of continual intoxication, was the judge before whom the lovely and innocent Paulina was now arraigned on a charge affecting her life. In fact, it became obvious that the process was not designed for any other purpose than to save appearances, and, if that should seem possible, to extract further discoveries from the prisoner. The general acted as supreme arbiter in every question of rights and power that arose to the court in the administration of their almost unlimited functions. Doubts he allowed of none; and cut every knot of jurisprudence, whether form or substance, by his Croatian sabre. Two assessors, however, he willingly received upon his bench of justice, to relieve him from the fatigue and difficulty of conducting a perplexed examination.

These assessors were lawyers of a low class, who tempered the exercise of their official duties with as few scruples of justice, and as little regard to the restraints of courtesy, as their military principal. The three judges were almost equally ferocious, and tools equally abject of the unprincipled sovereign whom they served.

A sovereign, however, he was; and Paulina was well aware that in his own states he had the power of life and death. She had good reason to see that her own death was resolved on; still she neglected no means of honorable self-defence. In a tone of mingled sweetness and dignity she maintained her innocence of all that was alleged against her; protested that she was unacquainted with the tenor of any papers which might have been found in her trunks; and claimed her privilege, as a subject of the emperor, in bar of all right on the Landgrave's part to call her to account. These pleas were overruled, and when she further acquainted the court that she was a near relative of the emperor's, and ventured to hint at the vengeance with which his imperial majesty would not fail to visit so bloody a contempt of justice, she was surprised to find this menace treated with mockery and laughter. In reality, the long habit of fighting for and against all the princes of Germany had given to the Croatian general a disregard for any of them, except on the single consideration of receiving his pay at the moment; and a single circumstance, unknown to Paulina, in the final determination of the Landgrave, to earn a merit with his Swedish allies by breaking off all terms of reserve and compromise with the imperial court, impressed a savage desperation on the tone of that prince's policy at this particular time. The Landgrave had resolved to stake his all upon a single throw. A battle was now expected, which, if favorable to the Swedes, would lay open the road to Vienna. The Landgrave was prepared to abide the issue; not, perhaps, wholly uninfluenced to so extreme a course by the very paper which had been robbed from Paulina. His policy was known to his agents, and conspicuously influenced their manner of receiving her menace.

Menaces, they informed her, came with better grace
from those who had the power to enforce them; and,
with a brutal scoff, the Croatian bade her merit their
indulgence by frank discoveries and voluntary confessions. He insisted on knowing the nature of the connection which the imperial colonel of horse, Maximilian, had maintained with the students of Klosterheim;
and upon other discoveries, with respect to most of
which Paulina was too imperfectly informed herself to
be capable of giving any light. Her earnest declarations
to this effect were treated with disregard. She was dismissed for the present, but with an intimation that on
the morrow she must prepare herself with a more com-
plying temper, or with a sort of firmness in maintaining
her resolution, which would not, perhaps, long resist
those means which the law had placed at their disposal
for dealing with the refractory and obstinate.

CHAPTER XXIV

PAULINA meditated earnestly upon the import of this
parting threat. The more she considered it, the less
could she doubt that these fierce inquisitors had meant
to threaten her with torture. She felt the whole indignity
of such a threat, though she could hardly bring herself
to believe them in earnest.

On the following morning she was summoned early
before her judges. They had not yet assembled; but
some of the lower officials were pacing up and down,
exchanging unintelligible jokes, looking sometimes at
herself, sometimes at an iron machine, with a complex
arrangement of wheels and screws. Dark were the suspicions which assaulted Paulina as this framework or
couch of iron first met her eyes; and perhaps some of

the jests circulating amongst the brutal ministers of her brutal judges would have been intelligible enough, had she condescended to turn her attention in that direction. Meantime her doubts were otherwise dispersed. The Croatian officer now entered the room alone, his assessors having probably declined participation in that part of the horrid functions which remained under the Landgrave's commission.

This man, presenting a paper with a long list of interrogatories to Paulina, bade her now rehearse verbally the sum of the answers which she designed to give. Running rapidly through them, Paulina replied, with dignity, yet trembling and agitated, that these were questions which in any sense she could not answer; many of them referring to points on which she had no knowledge, and none of them being consistent with the gratitude and friendship so largely due on her side to the persons implicated in the bearing of these questions.

"Then you refuse?"

"Certainly; there are three questions only which it is in my power to answer at all—even these imperfectly. Answers such as you expect would load me with dishonor."

"Then you refuse?"

"For the reasons I have stated, undoubtedly I do."

"Once more—you refuse?"

"I refuse, certainly; but do me the justice to record my reasons."

"Reasons!—ha! ha! they had need to be strong ones if they will hold out against the arguments of this pretty plaything," laying his hand upon the machine. "However, the choice is yours, not mine."

So saying, he made a sign to the attendants. One began to move the machine, and work the screws, or raise the clanking grates and framework, with a savage din; two others bared their arms. Paulina looked on motionless with sudden horror, and palpitating with fear.

The Croatian nodded to the men, and then, in a loud, commanding voice, exclaimed, "The question in the first degree!"

At this moment Paulina recovered her strength, which the first panic had dispelled. She saw a man approach her with a ferocious grin of exultation. Another, with the same horrid expression of countenance, carried a large vase of water.

The whole indignity of the scene flashed full upon her mind. She, a lady of the imperial house, threatened with torture by the base agent of a titled ruffian! She, who owed him no duty,—had violated no claim of hospitality, though in her own person all had been atrociously outraged!

Thoughts like these flew rapidly through her brain, when suddenly a door opened behind her. It was an attendant with some implements for tightening or relaxing bolts. The bare-armed ruffian at this moment raised his arm to seize hers. Shrinking from the pollution of his accursed touch, Paulina turned hastily round, darted through the open door, and fled, like a dove pursued by vultures, along the passages which stretched before her. Already she felt their hot breathing upon her neck, already the foremost had raised his hand to arrest her, when a sudden turn brought her full upon a band of young women, tending upon one of superior rank, manifestly their mistress.

"O, madam!" exclaimed Paulina, "save me! save me!" and with these words fell exhausted at the lady's feet.

This female—young, beautiful, and with a touching pensiveness of manners—raised her tenderly in her arms, and with a sisterly tone of affection bade her fear nothing; and the respectful manner in which the officials retired at her command satisfied Paulina that she stood in some very near relation to the Land-grave,—in reality, she soon spoke of him as her father. "Is it possible," thought Paulina to herself, "that this innocent and lovely child (for she was not more than seventeen, though with a prematurity of womanly person that raised her to a level with Paulina's height) should owe the affection of a daughter to a tyrant so savage as the Landgrave?"

She found, however, that the gentle Princess Adeline owed to her own childlike simplicity the best gift that one so situated could have received from the bounty of Heaven. The barbarities exercised by the Croatian governor she charged entirely upon his own brutal nature; and so confirmed was she in this view by Paulina's own case, that she now resolved upon executing a resolution she had long projected. Her father's confidence was basely abused; this she said, and devoutly believed. "No part of the truth ever reached him; her own letters remained disregarded in a way which was irreconcilable with the testimonies of profound affection to herself, daily showered upon her by his highness."

In reality, this sole child of the Landgrave was also the one sole jewel that gave a value in his eyes to his else desolate life. Everything in and about the castle of Lovenstein was placed under her absolute control; even the brutal Croatian governor knew that no plea or extremity of circumstances would atone for one act of disobedience to her orders; and hence it was that the ministers of this tyrant retired with so much prompt obedience to her commands.

Experience, however, had taught the princess that, not unfrequently, orders apparently obeyed were afterwards secretly evaded; and the disregard paid of late to her letters of complaint satisfied her that they were stifled and suppressed by the governor. Paulina, therefore, whom a few hours of unrestrained intercourse had made interesting to her heart, she would not suffer even to sleep apart from herself. Her own agitation on the poor prisoner's behalf became greater even than that of Paulina; and as fresh circumstances of suspicion daily arose in the savage governor's deportment, she now took in good earnest those measures for escape to Klosterheim which she had long arranged. In this purpose she was greatly assisted by the absolute authority which her father had conceded to her over everything but the mere military arrangements in the fortress. Under the color of an excursion, such as she had been daily accustomed to take, she found no difficulty in placing Paulina, sufficiently disguised, amongst her own servants. At a proper point of the road, Paulina and a few attendants, with the princess herself, issued from their coaches, and, bidding them await their return in half an hour's interval, by that time were far advanced upon their road to the military post of Falkenberg.

CHAPTER XXV

In twenty days the mysterious Masque had summoned the Landgrave "to answer for crimes unatoned, before a tribunal where no power but that of innocence could avail him." These days were nearly expired. The morning of the twentieth had arrived.

There were two interpretations of this summons. By many it was believed that the tribunal contemplated was that of the emperor; and that, by some mysterious plot, which could not be more difficult of execution than others which had actually been accomplished by The Masque, on this day the Landgrave would be carried off to Vienna. Others, again, understanding by the tribunal, in the same sense, the imperial chamber of criminal justice, believed it possible to fulfil the summons in some way less liable to delay or uncertainty than by a long journey to Vienna, through a country beset with enemies. But a third party, differing from both the others, understood by the tribunal where innocence was the only shield the judgment-seat of heaven; and believed that on this day justice would be executed on the Landgrave, for crimes known and unknown, by a public and memorable death. Under any interpretation, however, nobody amongst the citizens could venture peremptorily to deny, after the issue of the masqued ball, and of so many other public denunciations, that The Masque would keep his word to the letter.

It followed, of necessity, that everybody was on the tiptoe of suspense, and that the interest hanging upon the issue of this night's events swallowed up all other anxieties, of whatsoever nature. Even the battle which was now daily expected between the imperial and Swedish armies ceased to occupy the hearts and conversation of the citizens. Domestic and public concerns alike gave way to the coming catastrophe so solemnly denounced by The Masque.

The Landgrave alone maintained a gloomy reserve, and the expression of a haughty disdain. He had resolved to meet the summons with the liveliest expression of defiance, by fixing this evening for a second masqued ball, upon a greater scale than the first. In doing this he acted advisedly, and with the counsel of his Swedish allies. They represented to him that the issue of the approaching battle might be relied upon as pretty nearly certain; all the indications were indeed generally thought to promise a decisive turn in their favor; but, in the worst case, no defeat of the Swedish army in this war had ever been complete; that the bulk of the retreating army, if the Swedes should be obliged to retreat, would

take the road to Klosterheim, and would furnish to himself a garrison capable of holding the city for many
months to come (and *that* would ..ot fail to bring many
fresh chances to all of them), whilst to his new and cor-
dial allies this course would offer a secure retreat from
pursuing enemies, and a satisfactory proof of his own
fidelity. This even in the worst case, whereas in the better and more probable one, of a victory to the Swedes, to
maintain the city but for a day or two longer against
internal conspirators, and the secret cooperators outside, would be in effect to ratify any victory which the
Swedes might gain by putting into their hands at a critical moment one of its most splendid trophies and
guarantees.

These counsels fell too much into the Landgrave's
own way of thinking to meet with any demurs from him.
It was agreed, therefore, that as many Swedish troops as
could at this important moment be spared should be
introduced into the halls and saloons of the castle, on
the eventful evening, disguised as masquers. These
were about four hundred; and other arrangements
were made, equally mysterious, and some of them
known only to the Landgrave.

At seven o'clock, as on the former occasion, the company began to assemble. The same rooms were thrown
open; but, as the party was now far more numerous,
and was made more comprehensive in point of rank, in
order to include all who were involved in the conspiracy
which had been some time maturing in Klosterheim,
fresh suites of rooms were judged necessary, on the
pretext of giving fuller effect to the princely hospitalities of the Landgrave. And, on this occasion, according to an old privilege conceded in the case of corona-
tions or galas of magnificence, by the lady abbess of St.
Agnes, the partition walls were removed between the
great hall of the *schloss* and the refectory of that im-

mense convent; so that the two vast establishments, which on one side were contiguous to each other, were thus laid into one.

The company had now continued to pour in for two hours. The palace and the refectory of the convent were now overflowing with lights and splendid masques; the avenues and corridors rang with music; and, though every heart was throbbing with fear and suspense, no outward expression was wanting of joy and festal pleasure. For the present, all was calm around the slumbering volcano.

Suddenly, the Count St. Aldenheim, who was standing with arms folded, and surveying the brilliant scene, felt some one touch his hand, in the way concerted amongst the conspirators as a private signal of recognition. He turned, and recognized his friend the Baron Adelort, who saluted him with three emphatic words— "We are betrayed!"—Then, after a pause, "Follow me."

St. Aldenheim made his way through the glittering crowds, and pressed after his conductor into one of the most private corridors.

"Fear not," said the other, "that we shall be watched. Vigilance is no longer necessary to our crafty enemy. He has already triumphed. Every avenue of escape is barred and secured against us; every outlet of the palace is occupied by the Landgrave's troops. Not a man of us will return alive."

"Heaven forbid we should prove ourselves such gulls! You are but jesting, my friend."

"Would to God I were! my information is but too certain. Something I have overheard by accident; something has been told me; and something I have seen. Come you, also, Count, and see what I will show you: then judge for yourself."

So saying, he led St. Aldenheim by a little circuit of passages to a doorway, through which they passed into a hall of vast proportions; to judge by the catafalques, and mural monuments, scattered at intervals along the vast expanse of its walls, this seemed to be the ante-chapel of St. Agnes. In fact it was so; a few faint lights glimmered through the gloomy extent of this immense chamber, placed (according to the Catholic rite) at the shrine of the saint. Feeble as it was, however, the light was powerful enough to display in the centre a pile of scaffolding covered with black drapery. Standing at the foot, they could trace the outlines of a stage at the summit, fenced in with a railing, a block, and the other apparatus for the solemnity of a public execution, whilst the saw-dust below their feet ascertained the spot in which the heads were to fall.

"Shall we ascend and rehearse our parts?" asked the Count: "for methinks everything is prepared, except the headsman and the spectators. A plague on the inhospitable knave!"

"Yes, St. Aldenheim, all is prepared—even to the sufferers. On that list you stand foremost. Believe me, I speak with knowledge; no matter where gained. It is certain."

"Well, *necessitas non habet legem;* and he that dies on Tuesday will never catch cold on Wednesday. But, still, that comfort is something of the coldest. Think you that none better could be had?"

"As how?"

"Revenge, *par exemple;* a little revenge. Might one not screw the neck of this base prince, who abuses the confidence of cavaliers so perfidiously? To die I care not; but to be caught in a trap, and die like a rat lured by a bait of toasted cheese—Faugh! my countly blood rebels against it!"

"Something might surely be done, if we could muster in any strength. That is, we might die sword in hand; but—"

"Enough! I ask no more. Now let us go. We will separately pace the rooms, draw together as many of our
party as we can single out, and then proclaim ourselves.
Let each answer for one victim. I'll take his highness for
my share."

With this purpose, and thus forewarned of the dreadful fate at hand, they left the gloomy antechapel,
traversed the long suite of entertaining rooms, and collected as many as could easily be detached from the
dances without too much pointing out their own motions to the attention of all present. The Count St. Aldenheim was seen rapidly explaining to them the circumstances of their dreadful situation; whilst hands
uplifted, or suddenly applied to the hilt of the sword,
with other gestures of sudden emotion, expressed the
different impressions of rage or fear, which, under each
variety of character, impressed the several hearers.
Some of them, however, were too unguarded in their
motions; and the energy of their gesticulations had now
begun to attract the attention of the company.

The Landgrave himself had his eye upon them. But
at this moment his attention was drawn off by an uproar
of confusion in an ante-chamber, which argued some
tragical importance in the cause that could prompt so
sudden a disregard for the restraints of time and place.

CHAPTER XXVI

His highness issued from the room in consternation,
followed by many of the company. In the very centre of
the ante-room, booted and spurred, bearing all the
marks of extreme haste, panic, and confusion, stood a
Swedish officer, dealing forth hasty fragments of some
heart-shaking intelligence. "All is lost!" said he; "not a

regiment has escaped!" "And the place?" exclaimed a press of inquirers. "Nordlingen." "And which way has the Swedish army retreated?" demanded a masque behind him.

"Retreat!" retorted the officer, "I tell you there *is* no retreat. All have perished. The army is no more. Horse, foot, artillery—all is wrecked, crushed, annihilated. Whatever yet lives is in the power of the imperialists."

At this moment the Landgrave came up, and in every way strove to check these too liberal communications. He frowned; the officer saw him not. He laid his hand on the officer's arm, but all in vain. He spoke, but the officer knew not, or forgot his rank. Panic and immeasurable sorrow had crushed his heart; he cared not for restraints; decorum and ceremony were become idle words. The Swedish army had perished. The greatest disaster of the whole Thirty Years' War had fallen upon his countrymen. His own eyes had witnessed the tragedy, and he had no power to check or restrain that which made his heart overflow.

The Landgrave retired. But in half an hour the banquet was announced; and his highness had so much command over his own feelings that he took his seat at the table. He seemed tranquil in the midst of general agitation; for the company were distracted by various passions. Some exulted in the great victory of the imperialists, and the approaching liberation of Klosterheim. Some, who were in the secret, anticipated with horror the coming tragedy of vengeance upon his enemies which the Landgrave had prepared for this night. Some were filled with suspense and awe on the probable fulfilment in some way or other, doubtful as to the mode, but tragic (it was not doubted) for the result, of The Masque's mysterious denunciation.

Under such circumstances of universal agitation and suspense,—for on one side or other it seemed inevitable that this night must produce a tragical catastrophe,—it was not extraordinary that silence and embarrassment should at one moment take possession of the company, and at another that kind of forced and intermitting gayety which still more forcibly proclaimed the trepidation which really mastered the spirits of the assemblage. The banquet was magnificent; but it moved heavily and in sadness. The music, which broke the silence at intervals, was animating and triumphant; but it had no power to disperse the gloom which hung over the evening, and which was gathering strength conspicuously as the hours advanced to midnight.

As the clock struck eleven, the orchestra had suddenly become silent; and, as no buzz of conversation succeeded, the anxiety of expectation became more painfully irritating. The whole vast assemblage was hushed, gazing at the doors, at each other, or watching, stealthily, the Landgrave's countenance. Suddenly a sound was heard in an ante-room; a page entered with a step hurried and discomposed, advanced to the Landgrave's seat, and, bending downwards, whispered some news or message to that prince, of which not a syllable could be caught by the company. Whatever were its import, it could not be collected, from any very marked change on the features of him to whom it was addressed, that he participated in the emotions of the messenger, which were obviously those of grief or panic— perhaps of both united. Some even fancied that a transient expression of malignant exultation crossed the Landgrave's countenance at this moment. But, if that were so, it was banished as suddenly; and, in the next instant, the prince arose with a leisurely motion; and, with a very successful affectation (if such it were) of extreme tranquillity, he moved forwards to one of the ante-rooms, in which, as it now appeared, some person was awaiting his presence.

Who, and on what errand? These were the questions which now racked the curiosity of those among the company who had least concern in the final event, and more painfully interested others, whose fate was consciously dependent upon the accidents which the next hour might happen to bring up. Silence still continuing to prevail, and, if possible, deeper silence than before, it was inevitable that all the company, those even whose honorable temper would least have brooked any settled purpose of surprising the Landgrave's secrets, should, in some measure, become a party to what was now passing in the ante-room.

The voice of the Landgrave was heard at times, briefly and somewhat sternly in reply, but apparently in the tone of one who is thrown upon the necessity of self-defence. On the other side, the speaker was earnest, solemn, and (as it seemed) upon an office of menace or upbraiding. For a time, however, the tones were low and subdued; but, as the passion of the scene advanced, less restraint was observed on both sides; and at length many believed that in the stranger's voice they recognized that of the lady abbess; and it was some corroboration of this conjecture, that the name of Paulina began now frequently to be caught, and in connection with ominous words, indicating some dreadful fate supposed to have befallen her.

A few moments dispersed all doubts. The tones of bitter and angry reproach rose louder than before; they were, without doubt, those of the abbess. She charged the blood of Paulina upon the Landgrave's head; denounced the instant vengeance of the emperor for so great an atrocity; and, if that could be evaded, bade him expect certain retribution from Heaven for so wanton and useless an effusion of innocent blood.

The Landgrave replied in a lower key; and his words were few and rapid. That they were words of fierce recrimination, was easily collected from the tone; and in the next minute the parties separated with little ceremony (as was sufficiently evident) on either side, and with mutual wrath. The Landgrave reëntered the banqueting-room; his features discomposed and inflated with passion; but such was his self-command, and so habitual his dissimulation, that, by the time he reached his seat, all traces of agitation had disappeared; his countenance had resumed its usual expression of stern serenity, and his manners their usual air of perfect self-possession.

———

The clock of St. Agnes struck twelve. At that sound the Landgrave rose. "Friends and illustrious strangers!" said he, "I have caused one seat to be left empty for that blood-stained Masque, who summoned me to answer on' this night for a crime which he could not name, at a bar which no man knows. His summons you heard. Its fulfilment is yet to come. But I suppose few of us are weak enough to expect—"

"That The Masque of Klosterheim will ever break his engagements," said a deep voice, suddenly interrupting the Landgrave. All eyes were directed to the sound; and, behold! there stood The Masque, and seated himself quietly in the chair which had been left vacant for his reception.

"It is well!" said the Landgrave; but the air of vexation and panic with which he sank back into his seat belied his words. Rising again, after a pause, with some agitation, he said, "Audacious criminal! since last we met, I have learned to know you, and to appreciate your purposes. It is now fit they should be known to Klosterheim.

A scene of justice awaits you at present, which will teach this city to understand the delusions which could build any part of her hopes upon yourself. Citizens and friends, not I, but these dark criminals and interlopers whom you will presently see revealed in their true colors, are answerable for that interruption to the course of our peaceful festivities, which will presently be brought before you. Not I, but they are responsible."

So saying, the Landgrave arose, and the whole of the immense audience, who now resumed their masques, and prepared to follow whither his highness should lead. With the haste of one who fears he may be anticipated in his purpose, and the fury of some bird of prey, apprehending that his struggling victim may be yet torn from his talons, the prince hurried onwards to the antechapel. Innumerable torches now illuminated its darkness; in other respects it remained as St. Aldenheim had left it.

The Swedish masques had many of them withdrawn from the gala on hearing the dreadful day of Nordlingen. But enough remained, when strengthened by the body-guard of the Landgrave, to make up a corps of nearly five hundred men. Under the command of Colonel von Aremberg, part of them now enclosed the scaffold, and part prepared to seize the persons who were pointed out to them as conspirators. Amongst these stood foremost The Masque.

Shaking off those who attempted to lay hands upon him, he strode disdainfully within the ring; and then, turning to the Landgrave, he said—

"Prince, for once be generous; accept me as a ransom for the rest."

The Landgrave smiled sarcastically. "That were an unequal bargain, methinks, to take a part in exchange for the whole."

"The whole? And where is, then, your assurance of the whole?"

"Who should now make it doubtful? There is the block; the headsman is at hand. What hand can deliver from this extremity even you, Sir Masque?"

"That which has many times delivered me from a greater. It seems, prince, that you forget the last days in the history of Klosterheim. He that rules by night in Klosterheim may very well expect a greater favor than this when he descends to sue for it."

The Landgrave smiled contemptuously. "But, again I ask you, sir, will you on any terms grant immunity to these young men?"

"You sue as vainly for others as you would do for yourself."

"Then all grace is hopeless?" The Landgrave vouchsafed no answer, but made signals to Von Aremberg.

"Gentlemen, cavaliers, citizens of Klosterheim, you that are not involved in the Landgrave's suspicions," said The Masque, appealingly, "will you not join me in the intercession I offer for these young friends, who are else to perish unjudged, by blank edict of martial law?"

The citizens of Klosterheim interceded with ineffectual supplication. "Gentlemen, you waste your breath—they die without reprieve," replied the Landgrave.

"Will your highness spare none?"

"Not one," he exclaimed, angrily,—"not the youngest amongst them."

"Nor grant a day's respite to him who may appear, on examination, the least criminal of the whole?"

"A day's respite? No, nor half an hour's. Headsman, be ready. Soldiers, lay the heads of the prisoners ready for the axe."

"Detested prince, now look to your own!"

With a succession of passions flying over his face,—rage, disdain, suspicion,—the Landgrave looked round upon The Masque as he uttered these words, and, with pallid, ghastly consternation, beheld him raise to his lips a hunting-horn which depended from his neck. He blew a blast, which was immediately answered from within. Silence as of the grave ensued. All eyes were turned in the direction of the answer. Expectation was at its summit; and in less than a minute solemnly uprose the curtain, which divided the chapel from the ante-chapel, revealing a scene that smote many hearts with awe, and the consciences of some with as much horror as if it had really been that final tribunal which numbers believed The Masque to have denounced.

CHAPTER XXVII

The great chapel of St. Agnes, the immemorial hall of coronation for the Landgraves of X——, was capable of containing with ease from seven to eight thousand spectators. Nearly that number was now collected in the galleries, which, on the recurrence of that great occasion, or of a royal marriage, were usually assigned to the spectators. These were all equipped in burnished arms, the very *élite* of the imperial army. Resistance was hopeless; in a single moment the Landgrave saw himself dispossessed of all his hopes by an overwhelming force; the advanced guard, in fact, of the victorious imperialists, now fresh from Nordlingen.

On the marble area of the chapel, level with their own position, were arranged a brilliant staff of officers; and, a little in advance of them, so as almost to reach the ante-chapel, stood the imperial legate or ambassador. This nobleman advanced to the crowd of Klosterheimers, and spoke thus:

"Citizens of Klosterheim, I bring you from the emperor your true and lawful Landgrave, Maximilian, son of your last beloved prince."

Both chapels resounded with acclamations; and the troops presented arms.

"Show us our prince! let us pay him our homage!" echoed from every mouth.

"This is mere treason!" exclaimed the usurper. "The emperor invites treason against his own throne, who undermines that of other princes. The late Landgrave had no son; so much is known to you all."

"None that was known to his murderer," replied The Masque, "else had he met no better fate than his unhappy father."

"Murderer! And what art thou, blood-polluted Masque, with hands yet reeking from the blood of all who refused to join the conspiracy against your lawful prince?"

"Citizens of Klosterheim," said the legate, "first let the emperor's friend be assoiled from all injurious thoughts. Those whom ye believe to have been removed by murder are here to speak for themselves."

Upon this the whole line of those who had mysteriously disappeared from Klosterheim presented themselves to the welcome of their astonished friends.

"These," said the legate, "quitted Klosterheim, even by the same secret passages which enabled us to enter it, and for the self-same purpose,—to prepare the path for the restoration of the true heir, Maximilian the Fourth, whom in this noble prince you behold, and whom may God long preserve!"

Saying this, to the wonder of the whole assembly, he led forward The Masque, whom nobody had yet suspected for more than an agent of the true heir.

The Landgrave, meantime, thus suddenly denounced as a tyrant, usurper, murderer, had stood aloof, and had given but a slight attention to the latter words of the legate. A race of passions had traversed his countenance, chasing each other in flying succession. But by a prodigious effort he recalled himself to the scene before him; and, striding up to the crowd, of which the legate was the central figure, he raised his arm with a gesture of indignation, and protested vehemently that the assassination of Maximilian's father had been iniquitously charged upon himself.—"And yet," said he, "upon that one gratuitous assumption have been built all the other foul suspicions directed against my person."

"Pardon me, sir," replied the legate, "the evidences were such as satisfied the emperor and his council; and he showed it by the vigilance with which he watched over the Prince Maximilian, and the anxiety with which he kept him from approaching your highness, until his pretensions could be established by arms. But, if more direct evidence were wanting, since yesterday we have had it in the dying confession of the very agent employed to strike the fatal blow. That man died last night, penitent and contrite, having fully unburdened his conscience, at Waldenhausen. With evidence so overwhelming, the emperor exacts no further sacrifice from your highness than that of retirement from public life, to any one of your own castles in your patrimonial principality of Oberhornstein.—But, now for a more pleasing duty. Citizens of Klosterheim, welcome your young Landgrave in the emperor's name: and to-morrow you shall welcome also your future Landgravine, the lovely Countess Paulina, cousin to the emperor, my master, and cousin also to your noble young Landgrave."

"No!" exclaimed the malignant usurper, "her you shall never see alive; for that, be well assured, I have taken care."

"Vile, unworthy prince!" replied Maximilian, his eyes kindling with passion, "know that your intentions, so worthy of a fiend, towards that most innocent of ladies, have been confounded and brought to nothing by your own gentle daughter, worthy of a far nobler father."

"If you speak of my directions for administering the torture,—a matter in which I presume that I exercised no unusual privilege amongst German sovereigns,—you are right. But it was not that of which I spoke."

"Of what else, then?—The Lady Paulina has escaped."

"True, to Falkenberg. But, doubtless, young Landgrave, you have heard of such a thing as the intercepting of a fugitive prisoner; in such a case, you know the punishment which martial law awards. The governor at Falkenberg had his orders." These last significant words he uttered in a tone of peculiar meaning. His eye sparkled with bright gleams of malice and of savage vengeance, rioting in its completion.

"O, heart—heart!" exclaimed Maximilian, "can this be possible?"

The imperial legate and all present crowded around him to suggest such consolation as they could. Some offered to ride off express to Falkenberg; some argued that the Lady Paulina had been seen within the last hour. But the hellish exulter in ruined happiness destroyed that hope as soon as it dawned.

"Children!" said he, "foolish children! cherish not such chimeras. Me you have destroyed, Landgrave, and the prospects of my house. Now perish yourself.—Look there: is that the form of one who lives and breathes?"

All present turned to the scaffold, in which direction he pointed, and now first remarked, covered with a black pall, and brought hither doubtless to aggravate the pangs of death to Maximilian, what seemed but too certainly a female corpse. The stature, the fine swell of the bust, the rich outline of the form, all pointed to the same conclusion; and, in this recumbent attitude, it seemed but too clearly to present the magnificent proportions of Paulina.

There was a dead silence. Who could endure to break

it? Who make the effort which was forever to fix the fate of Maximilian?

He himself could not. At last the deposed usurper, craving for the consummation of his vengeance, himself strode forward; with one savage grasp he tore away the pall, and below it lay the innocent features, sleeping in her last tranquil slumber, of his own gentle-minded daughter!

———

No heart was found savage enough to exult; the sorrow even of such a father was sacred. Death, and through his own orders, had struck the only being whom he had ever loved; and the petrific mace of the fell destroyer seemed to have smitten his own heart, and withered its hopes forever.

Everybody comprehended the mistake in a moment. Paulina had lingered at Waldenhausen under the protection of an imperial corps, which she had met in her flight. The tyrant, who had heard of her escape, but apprehended no necessity for such a step on the part of his daughter, had issued sudden orders to the officer commanding the military post at Falkenberg, to seize and shoot the female prisoner escaping from confinement, without allowing any explanations whatsoever, on her arrival at Falkenberg. This precaution he had adopted in part to intercept any denunciation of the emperor's vengeance which Paulina might address to the officer. As a rude soldier, accustomed to obey the letter of his orders, this commandant had executed his commission; and the gentle Adeline, who had naturally hastened to the protection of her father's chateau, surrendered her breath meekly and with resignation to what she believed a simple act of military violence; and this she did before she could know a syllable of her father's guilt or his fall, and without any the least reason for supposing him connected with the occasion of her early death.

At this moment Paulina made her appearance unexpectedly, to reassure the young Landgrave by her presence, and to weep over her young friend, whom she had lost almost before she had come to know her. The scaffold, the corpse, and the other images of sorrow, were then withdrawn; seven thousand imperial troops presented arms to the youthful Landgrave and the future Landgravine, the brilliant favorites of the emperor; the immense area of St. Agnes resounded with the congratulations of Klosterheim; and as the magnificent cortege moved off to the interior of the *schloss*, the swell of the coronation anthem rising in peals upon the ear from the choir of St. Agnes, and from the military bands of the imperial troops, awoke the promise of happier days, and of more equitable government, to the long-harassed inhabitants of Klosterheim.

———

The Klosterheimers knew enough already, personally or by questions easily answered in every quarter, to supply any links which were wanting in the rapid explanations of the legate. Nevertheless, that nothing might remain liable to misapprehension or cavil, a short manifesto was this night circulated by the new government, from which the following facts are abstracted:

The last rightful Landgrave, whilst yet a young man, had been assassinated in the forest when hunting. A year or two before this catastrophe he had contracted what, from the circumstances, was presumed, at the time, to be a *morganatic* or left-handed marriage, with a lady of high birth, nearly connected with the imperial house. The effect of such a marriage went to incapacitate the children who might be born under it, male or female, from succeeding. On that account, as well as because current report had represented her as childless, the widow lady escaped all attempts from the assassin. Meantime this lady, who was no other than Sister Madeline, had been thus indebted for her safety to two rumors, which were in fact equally false. She soon found means of convincing the emperor, who had been the bosom friend of her princely husband, that her marriage was a perfect one, and conferred the fullest rights of succession upon her infant son Maximilian, whom at the earliest age, and with the utmost secrecy, she had committed to the care of his imperial majesty. This powerful guardian had in every way watched over the interests of the young prince. But the Thirty Years' War had thrown all Germany into distractions, which for a time thwarted the emperor, and favored the views of the usurper. Latterly, also, another question had arisen on the city and dependences of Klosterheim, as distinct from the Landgraviate. These, it was now affirmed, were a female appanage, and could only pass back to the Landgraves of X——through a marriage with the female inheretrix. To reconcile all claims, therefore, on finding this bar in the way, the emperor had resolved to promote a marriage for Maximilian with Paulina, who stood equally related to the imperial house and to that of her lover. In this view he had despatched Paulina to Klosterheim, with proper documents to support the claims of both parties. Of these documents she had been robbed at Waldenhausen; and the very letter which was designed to introduce Maximilian as "the child and sole representative of the late murdered Landgrave," falling in this surreptitious way into the usurper's hand, had naturally misdirected his attacks to the person of Paulina.

For the rest, as regarded the mysterious movements

of The Masque, these were easily explained. Fear, and the exaggerations of fear, had done one half the work to his hands, by preparing people to fall easy dupes to the plans laid, and by increasing the romantic wonders of his achievements. Cooperation, also, on the part of the very students and others, who stood forward as the night-watch for detecting him had served The Masque no less powerfully. The appearances of deadly struggles had been arranged artificially to countenance the plot and to aid the terror. Finally, the secret passages which communicated between the forest and the chapel of St. Agnes (passages of which many were actually applied to that very use in the Thirty Years' War) had been unreservedly placed at their disposal by the lady abbess, an early friend of the unhappy Landgravine, who sympathized deeply with that lady's unmerited sufferings.

One other explanation followed, communicated in a letter from Maximilian to the legate; this related to the murder of the old seneschal,—a matter in which the young prince took some blame to himself, as having unintentionally drawn upon that excellent servant his unhappy fate. "The seneschal," said the writer, "was the faithful friend of my family, and knew the whole course of its misfortunes. He continued his abode at the *schloss*, to serve my interest; and in some measure I may fear that I drew upon him his fate. Traversing late one evening a suite of rooms, which his assistance and my own mysterious disguise laid open to my passage at all hours, I came suddenly upon the prince's retirement. He pursued me, but with hesitation. Some check I gave to his motions by halting before a portrait of my unhappy father, and emphatically pointing his attention to it. Conscience, I well knew, would supply a commentary to my act. I produced the impression which I had anticipated, but not so strongly as to stop his pursuit. My course necessarily drew him into the seneschal's room.

The old man was sleeping; and this accident threw into the prince's hands a paper, which, I have reason to think, shed some considerable light upon my own pretensions, and, in fact, first made my enemy acquainted with my existence and my claims. Meantime, the seneschal had secured the prince's vengeance upon himself. He was now known as a faithful agent in my service. That fact signed his death-warrant. There is a window in a gallery which commands the interior of the seneschal's room. On the evening of the last *fête*, waiting there for an opportunity of speaking securely with this faithful servant, I heard a deep groan, and then another, and another; I raised myself, and, with an ejaculation of horror, looked down upon the murderer, then surveying his victim with hellish triumph. My loud exclamation drew the murderer's eye upwards: under the pangs of an agitated conscience, I have reason to think that he took me for my unhappy father, who perished at my age, and is said to have resembled me closely. Who that murderer was, I need not say more directly. He fled with the terror of one who flies from an apparition. Taking a lesson from this incident, on that same night, by the very same sudden revelation of what passed, no doubt, for my father's countenance, aided by my mysterious character, and the proof I had announced to him immediately before my acquaintance with the secret of the seneschal's murder, in this and no other way it was that I produced that powerful impression upon the prince which terminated the festivities of that evening, and which all Klosterheim witnessed. If not, it is for the prince to explain in what other way I did or could affect him so powerfully."

This explanation of the else unaccountable horror manifested by the ex-Landgrave on the sudden exposure of The Masque's features, received a remarkable confirmation from the confession of the miserable assassin at Waldenhausen. This man's illness had been first brought on by the sudden shock of a situation pretty nearly the same, acting on a conscience more disturbed, and a more superstitious mind. In the very act of attempting to assassinate or rob Maximilian, he had been suddenly dragged by that prince into a dazzling light; and this settling full upon features which too vividly recalled to the murderer's recollection the last unhappy Landgrave, at the very same period of blooming manhood, and in his own favorite hunting palace, not far from which the murder had been perpetrated, naturally enough had for a time unsettled the guilty man's understanding, and, terminating in a nervous fever, had at length produced his penitential death.

A death, happily of the same character, soon overtook the deposed Landgrave. He was laid by the side of his daughter, whose memory, as much even as his own penitence, availed to gather round his final resting-place the forgiving thoughts even of those who had suffered most from his crimes. Klosterheim in the next age flourished greatly, being one of those cities which benefited by the peace of Westphalia. Many changes took place in consequence greatly affecting the architectural character of the town and its picturesque antiquities; but, amidst all revolutions of this nature, the secret passages still survive, and to this day are shown occasionally to strangers of rank and consideration, by which, more than by any other of the advantages at his disposal, The Masque of Klosterheim was enabled to replace himself in his patrimonial rights, and at the same time to liberate from a growing oppression his own compatriots and subjects.

3 9001 01436 5897